ABOUT THE AUTHOR

Judith Berrisford is well known for her pony stories which combine excitement and adventure with plenty of authentic detail about riding and pony keeping. This is her third book about the Brooke family and their ponies. The other two, both of which are available in Knight Books, are A PONY IN THE FAMILY and A COLT IN THE FAMILY

Judith Berrisford lives with her husband on the North Wales coast, where they can enjoy their outdoor interests in dogs, horses, swimming, birdwatching and gardening.

'All one should know about pony-keeping in a family atmosphere is here'

Time and Tide

A Show Jumper in the Family

Judith Berrisford

Illustrated by Anne Gordon

KNIGHT BOOKS
Hodder and Stoughton

To Adrian Charles Brown, Suzanne Elizabeth Brown, Denise
Ann Shirley, Debra Mary Brown, Barry Andrew Shirley for
having such wonderful grandparents

Text copyright © 1964 Judith M. Berrisford
Illustrations copyright © 1964 Brockhampton Press Ltd

First published by Brockhampton Press Ltd 1964
Knight Books edition 1978
Third impression 1982

Printed and bound in Great Britain for
Hodder & Stoughton Paperbacks, a
division of Hodder and Stoughton Ltd,
Mill Road, Dunton Green, Sevenoaks,
Kent (Editorial Office: 47 Bedford
Square, London, WC1 3DP) by
Hazell Watson & Viney Ltd,
Aylesbury, Bucks

ISBN 0 340 21657 3

Contents

To
Adrian Charles Brown
Suzanne Elizabeth Brown
Denise Ann Shirley
Debra Mary Brown
Barry Andrew Shirley
    for having such wonderful grandparents

ONE

Daddy says 'No'

'Now just a minute, Janey!' Mr Brooke looked up from his apple-pie and gazed seriously across the lunch table at his elder daughter. 'When I agreed to you and Penny having ponies, I hadn't bargained for your wanting to take up show jumping.'

'But, Daddy,' Jane protested. 'Most people with ponies want to do a bit of show jumping.'

'I certainly do,' added Penny, 'because Rusty could be really good.' She turned to her mother. 'You believe in Rusty, don't you, Mummy? Can't you persuade Daddy?'

'Why should I?' Mrs Brooke was firm. 'I agree with him. We're not made of money, and it seems to me that there's no end to your pony demands. First you persuade Daddy to buy you Freckles; then Penny gets given Bramble and you talk us into letting you keep *two* ponies. Next, Penny grows out of Bramble and you want to change him for Rusty.'

'And worry your mother out of her wits while you're breaking him in,' put in Mr Brooke.

'But it all turned out right in the end.' Penny looked from one of her parents to the other. 'Rusty's quite a steady pony now, and he is going to be a simply super jumper.'

'You should have seen him in the jumping lane this morning,' added Jane. 'That pony really can *jump*.'

Mr Brooke groaned. 'Now listen, you two,' he said. 'Your mother and I aren't spoil-sports, and if you want Rusty to jump, we won't stop you, as long as you take care and don't break any bones. But forget about show jumping because, as your mother says, we can't afford it.'

Penny and Jane looked downcast.

'Come on—cheer up!' Mr Brooke urged. 'You can still have plenty of fun jumping in the field. But don't build up hopes about show jumping or imagine you can coax me to change my mind. There's going to be no show jumping in this family, and that's definite.'

'Well, I suppose that's that,' Penny said to Jane a few minutes later when they were in the kitchen putting on their aprons and getting ready to do the washing up. 'It's a pity.' She filled the plastic bowl with hot water and squirted in some dish-washing fluid. 'But I suppose we're lucky that Mummy and Daddy will let us do a bit of jumping in the field.'

'Yes,' said Jane, 'let's start as soon as we've finished the dishes.'

Tea-towel in hand, she paused to wave through the window as her mother got beside her father into the van which bore the lettering 'G. BROOKE—Television and Radio. Easy Terms and Prompt Repairs.'

Jane sighed. Mummy and Daddy did have to work hard. Saturday afternoon was particularly busy in the shop since Daddy had started to sell 'pop' discs. He had installed listening booths and teenagers flocked into the shop to hear their favourites. Mummy was run off her feet.

After the dishes were dried, Jane and Penny got their bridles and saddles from the cupboard under the stairs and went out to the field. Both ponies were grazing, and Freckles was the first to hear the girls coming. She lifted her pretty tan-flecked grey head, gave a whinny of greeting and trotted across to the gate to meet them.

Rusty followed her, his russet tail carried high, his neat ears pricked and the heart-shaped patch of white on his forehead snowy against the smooth chestnut of his face. He looked every inch a jumper, close-coupled, with a strong short back and powerful hocks. There was 'spring' in every line of him.

Jane and Penny put a rope round each of their ponies' necks, looped it through the D's of their head-collars and tied the ponies with a non-slip, quick-release knot to the fence. They brushed off the mud and cleaned out Freckles' and Rusty's feet. Then, leaving the ponies tied up, they went to the garage to fetch the cavalletti that they had used two summers ago when Jane had first taught Freckles to jump.

The cavalletti consisted of six-foot long larch poles, nailed to crossed ends which could be turned round to vary the height.

The girls carried one of the cavalletti to the middle of the

9

field and turned it to its lowest height, about six inches from the ground.

Penny looked at it in disappointment.

'Rusty can walk over that,' she pointed out. 'Aren't we going to jump anything bigger?'

'Not at first,' Jane explained. 'As a matter of fact we're not even going to jump at all—not yet. The idea is to make the ponies *trot* over the poles so that they learn where to put their feet and also to lower and stretch their heads.'

'I remember,' said Penny. 'It's a kind of suppling exercise, isn't it?'

Jane nodded. 'We've really got to go right back to the beginning because, although Rusty jumped a lot in the jumping lane, he's never been taught to jump with a rider on his back.'

The girls mounted, and Jane trotted Freckles towards the cavalletti. 'I'll go first,' she said over her shoulder to Penny, 'to give Rusty a lead. Don't forget, no jumping. Trotting only.'

Jane leaned forward and trotted Freckles smoothly at the very low pole.

The grey pony looked at it, and then lowered her head, and carefully trotted over. Freckles had done this before and she understood what was expected of her. On the other hand, this was the first time Rusty had ever seen the cavalletti. He fretted his bit, and sidled up to it.

'Go on, silly,' Penny urged, touching him with her heels. 'Over you go.'

Rusty stood stock-still. He looked at the cavalletti, and then, nostrils flaring with fright, took off in an enormous jump, clearing the pole with several feet to spare, and throwing Penny on to his neck.

'Whoa!' gasped Penny, struggling back into the saddle.

'What made you do that, Rusty?'

'He was so scared of the pole,' Jane said, trotting back, 'that he didn't want to risk touching it. We ought to have let him have a good look at it first.'

Penny dismounted, and led Rusty back to the cavalletti, allowing him to sniff and nose the pole.

'You see,' she said, patting him. 'It won't bite!'

She mounted again and rode Rusty after Jane who was once more trotting Freckles to the cavalletti. This time Rusty followed Freckles over without protest, trotting correctly but holding his feet very high in a comical way.

'Well done, Rusty,' Jane called over her shoulder. 'Follow me round in a circle, Penny, and we'll take them over again.'

Jane and Penny trotted Freckles and Rusty over the cavalletti four more times. Then they dismounted and put three more cavalletti, each five feet apart, to form a line down the middle of the field.

Jane gathered up Freckles' reins and remounted. Penny followed while Jane rode Freckles towards the line of cavalletti at a slow trot. Freckles went over them all, picking up her feet carefully, extending her neck, and looking the picture of a well-balanced, properly-schooled pony.

Freckles set a perfect example for Rusty. Penny thought — but the trouble was that Rusty did not seem to be paying enough attention. He was pulling at his bit. Sweat was breaking out on his neck, and he gave a couple of dancing steps sideways. It seemed as though even this slow progress was too exciting for the colt. He was 'hotting up'.

Penny slid to the ground and, running her stirrups up the leathers, pulled Rusty's reins over his head. 'I'll have to lead him over,' she called to Jane and, grasping Rusty's reins near the bit with her right hand, took the slack in her left and led him towards the cavalletti at a walk.

Now that Penny was leading him, Rusty seemed reassured. Carefully picking up his feet, he followed Penny over the cavalletti.

After twice leading him round, Penny broke into a run, and Rusty, anxious but sure-footed, negotiated the poles.

'So far, so good,' said Jane, watching. 'Now get back into the saddle and ride him over.'

Once Penny was on his back, however, Rusty seemed to think that the harmless cavalletti had become difficult and dangerous. Shying and digging in his toes, he refused to go over until, at last, Penny and Jane were forced to go back to using a single cavalletti and then adding just one more so that the ponies were trotting over two.

'Rusty seems supple enough,' said Jane, reining up Freckles at last, and eyeing Penny's pony critically, 'but he does "hot up".'

'Give him a chance,' said Penny, patting Rusty's neck. 'This is the first time he's jumped with a rider on his back. He's got to get used to the idea. Wait and see how he does tomorrow.'

TWO

Riding for a fall

NEXT day, Jane and Penny went back to the beginning, repeating Freckles' and Rusty's lesson over a single cavalletti, and then over two before adding a third. Rusty was still apt to get excited, and occasionally to jump the poles instead of trotting over them, which was all that Jane and Penny wanted him to do at this stage.

'He's still "hotting-up",' said Jane at the end of the practice.

'All the same,' said Penny, dismounting, 'he's making good progress.'

'Yes,' agreed Jane. 'But the trouble is that weekends are too short. If only we didn't have to go to school tomorrow he might make real headway.'

'School or not,' Penny said determinedly, 'I'm going to keep up Rusty's jumping.'

Despite school and homework, during the next week the two girls managed to give the ponies four pre-jumping lessons. Jane and Penny had persuaded their mother to let them have their tea a little later so that they could ride the ponies for half an hour as soon as they got off the bus.

By the end of the week Rusty was able to canter over four cavalletti without getting too excited or jumping any of them.

The following week Jane and Penny turned the cavalletti round so that the poles were about eighteen inches from the ground. Instead of trotting or cantering over the poles, the ponies were now jumping.

Having got used to taking the obstacles smoothly and easily, in their stride as it were, Freckles and Rusty went over the poles rhythmically, and Jane and Penny found it surprisingly easy to keep their seats. They were sitting slightly forward, as advised in the pony books they had read, and, by keeping their weight over the ponies' withers, they were managing not to get 'left behind' over the jumps.

'This is super!' Penny said happily. 'By Saturday Rusty and Freckles will be ready for a bigger jump.'

'Yes, we'll stand one of the cavalletti on top of another one,' Jane planned, 'and put a third in front to make a really interesting jump.'

'Roll on Saturday,' whooped Penny as her father's van bounced up the lane—a signal for them to unsaddle the ponies and get ready for tea.

On Saturday afternoon, Mr and Mrs Brooke had gone to the shop as usual. Jane and Penny were finishing the washing up when the telephone bell rang. Penny ran to answer it.

'It's for you, Jane,' she called. 'A girl from school wants to speak to you. Hilary Dawson. She's a prefect and captain of the hockey team! Whatever can she want?'

'Hello, Hilary.' Jane sounded puzzled as she spoke into the mouthpiece. She listened for a moment, and then went on: 'Oh dear! That is bad luck! . . . Yes, you are in a fix. Well, Penny and I were just going to give our ponies a jumping lesson . . . Of course I don't want to let the school down . . . Very well, Hilary, I'll meet the bus at the end of our lane.'

'What's happened?' Penny demanded as Jane put down the telephone.

'Hilary wants me to play for the second team in the match against Wincliffe High,' Jane explained, getting her hockey stick and boots from the cupboard under the stairs. 'She was in a bit of a flap. Muriel Ferris has ricked her ankle, and one of the reserves has got 'flu. So I've got to play right-inner.'

'What about the jumping?' Penny could not hide her disappointment. 'All week we've been looking forward to Saturday afternoon.'

'I know,' said Jane. 'I don't want to go, but Hilary says I mustn't let the school down. So I suppose that's that.'

'I suppose so,' Penny agreed doubtfully. 'It's the old, old problem. School or ponies? Which should come first?'

Jane had no time to answer. She was already on her way upstairs to get her hockey shorts and jersey, and a moment later dashed out of the house and down the path towards the cross-roads.

'I'll just about make it,' she gasped to Penny who was running alongside. 'Hilary said that the coach which is taking our team to Wincliffe would be stopping at the end of our lane in five minutes' time. Gosh! There it is . . . Sorry, Penny,' she added as she clambered on to the coach, 'you'll be able to carry on schooling Rusty over the cavalletti; and we'll make a bigger jump tomorrow.'

Penny felt suddenly alone as the coach disappeared round the bend. Mummy and Daddy were at the shop. Jane had gone, and—goodness!—just at this moment there did not seem to be any sign of life around Orchard Cottage. She stood at the bottom of the lane, looking round. No traffic on the road; no birds twittering in the hedge; not even a cow in sight in the neighbouring meadows—and where were Rusty and Freckles?

Penny whistled to break the silence as she walked up the lane. Her heart felt less heavy when she heard the thud of pony hooves and she saw Rusty's friendly head stretched over the hedge neighing to her.

Penny brightened as she pulled on her crash-cap, bridled and saddled Rusty and mounted. She rode him round the field at a trot, and then turned him towards the line of cavalletti. Rusty neatly jumped them, so Penny rode him on round the field and back again to the obstacles. This time Rusty's stride seemed to have lost its spring. He was hanging back; not up to his bit. His steps seemed to slow; then, just in front of the first of the cavalletti, he stopped, dug in his toes and refused to move.

'Come on, Rusty,' Penny coaxed, urging him with her heels.

Rusty obstinately stood still.

'Move, Rusty!' Penny was exasperated now, and she gave her pony a sharp kick.

But Rusty stood his ground, so Penny gave him a touch with her switch. Immediately Rusty spun round and trotted up the field to the corner farthest from the jumps. He shook his head, fighting Penny's pressure on the bit.

Penny sat tight. She kept her hands low to bring Rusty's

head down, and turned him sharply to ride him again at the jumps.

Holding his neck stiffly, Rusty allowed himself to be urged to an unwilling canter. He reached the cavalletti and suddenly swerved, throwing Penny half-way up his shoulder.

'Having trouble?' called a boy's voice from the lane as Penny struggled back into her saddle.

Penny looked round to see a boy of about Jane's age, with a crash-cap mostly hiding his dark hair. He was on the other side of the field gate mounted on a smart bay pony with a black mane and tail.

Penny knew the boy by sight. He was named Bernard Palmer. His parents had recently come to live at the Old Malt House on the other side of the village.

'Hello,' Penny said to the boy. 'I don't know what's the matter with Rusty today. I've been schooling him over these cavalletti for the past three weeks, and he's never refused before.'

'Perhaps he's getting bored,' said Bernard.

'Could be,' nodded Penny. 'Yes, I suppose it must be boring for him, going round and round over the cavalletti day after day instead of being taken for a ride in the lanes. Poor Rusty!'

She patted her pony's neck and trotted him to the gate. Both ponies lifted their heads, eyeing and sniffing at each other inquisitively.

'Rusty would have been tackling a proper jump today,' Penny told Bernard, and went on to relate how Jane had been called away to the hockey match just when they had been planning to build the cavalletti into a bigger jump.

'Hard luck,' said Bernard. 'But not to worry. Perhaps I can help. I've got a whole set of jumps in our paddock.' He opened the field gate for Penny to ride through. 'Bring Rusty along now if you like, and pop him over them.'

'Could I?' Penny's eyes shone. 'How super!'

Together they rode up the lane to the village. Rusty's ears were now pricked. He was holding his head high and his eyes looked bright and interested. He seemed to be enjoying the company of the other pony, and, as always, was pleased to be out of his field and seeing what was going on in the world beyond his hedge.

Soon they came in sight of the Old Malt House, and Penny caught her breath as she saw the seven or eight white-painted jumps, complete with wings, that had been laid out in the paddock behind the old honey-coloured stone house with its round malting tower. There were two brush-wood fences, a 'wall' of wooden bricks painted red with lighter edges to represent mortar. There was a triple-bar, an in-and-out, a stile, and a level-crossing with warning red

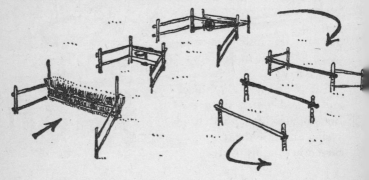

circles painted on the two parallel gates that made up the jump.

Penny was delighted. This was a real show jumping course. How wonderful that Bernard should have invited her and Rusty to try it.

Of course the jumps were bigger than she and Rusty had been jumping. They must be about three feet high. But that was all to the good, she told herself. Surely Rusty was ready for jumps of about this size.

Bernard opened the gate. 'I'll take Corker round first,' he suggested. 'So that Rusty can watch and get the idea.'

He cantered the bay pony to the first jump—one of the brushwood fences. Corker picked up his forefeet and sprang neatly off his hooks. He seemed to go over without any effort. So it was with all the jumps, Bernard and Corker just seemed to pop over them.

'See, Rusty.' Penny stroked her pony's neck. 'That's what you've got to do.' Rusty snatched at his bit. 'Don't get impatient,' Penny told him. 'It'll soon be your turn.'

But Rusty was impatient. In fact he was getting quite excited. Froth whitened the butt of his snaffle and he began to dance about.

'Raring to go, is he?' said Bernard, steadying Corker

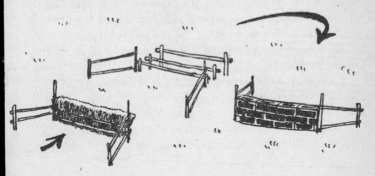

after landing over the last jump, and trotting back to Penny. 'Carry on. It's all yours.'

Rusty did not need Penny to give him the order to canter. As soon as she relaxed her pressure on his bit, he was off. A patch of sweat darkened his neck and he rocking-horsed his way to the jump. Pressing back his head and then thrusting it forward, he took off too soon, arched in a tremendous leap, and crashed through the brushwood with his forefeet bringing down the bar.

Penny tried to steady him before they approached the stile, but Rusty raced at it, took it much too fast, and knocked it over. He went round the course at a gallop, scattering the jumps with Penny, her cap askew, fighting to slow his pace. But it was all she could do to steer him towards the right jumps. However, as they neared the last obstacle—the wall —she did manage to get Rusty more under control. He took the wall at a steadier pace, but, with Penny trying to hold him back, he did not have enough impulsion to clear it, and knocked down the top row of bricks.

Ashamed, Penny rode back to Bernard who was waiting at the end of the paddock.

'Oh dear!' Penny sighed. 'We have disgraced ourselves.'

'Never mind,' said Bernard. 'I expect your pony's over-excited.' He moved towards the side of the course. 'Bring him to this schooling fence, and ride him over a few times to steady him before we pick up the jumps and try again.'

The schooling fence was a single post-and-rail about two feet six inches high.

'You ought to be able to jump this well enough, Rusty,' Penny told her colt, patting his chestnut neck. 'It's not really very much higher than your own cavalletti.'

She rode Rusty to the post-and-rail to let him have a good look at it. Then she turned, trotted him back up the field, swung him round and set him at the jump at a canter.

The obstacle looked simple enough to Penny, yet, to Rusty, it presented quite a problem. A single pole of that type was really quite the hardest fence for a pony to jump because, when a pony jumps, he focuses his gaze on the base of the fence, and that is how he judges his stride.

The post-and-rail had no pole or row of bricks for a base-line, and so Rusty could not judge where he should take off. He rose too late and knocked off the pole with his forefeet.

'Oh dear! We muffed that,' said Penny, not realizing the reason for Rusty's failure.

As Bernard replaced the pole, she rode Rusty at the jump again, taking it faster this time, and hoping that Rusty's speed would help him to clear it. But now the pole was a little higher and so it was even harder for Rusty to judge his take-off. This time he jumped too soon, and again blundered into the pole with his forefeet.

Bernard replaced the pole, and unnoticed by Penny, who was now riding Rusty up the field for another attempt, broke a thin switch from the hedge. He held it behind his back so that Rusty would not see it. Then, when the pony had taken off, he brought it forward and gave Rusty a sharp tap across his forefeet.

Rusty seemed to wince in mid air. He had barely landed before he began to buck. It was not the playful buck of a fresh pony working off his high spirits, but a determined effort to throw his rider.

Penny flew through the air to land with a thud that ricked her shoulder, and left her feeling dazed.

Rusty wheeled round. Putting his foot on his trailing reins and snapping them, he bolted, and despite Bernard's efforts to stop him, jumped the gate, and cantered home.

'Gosh!' said Bernard. 'I didn't expect him to do that.'

THREE

Pony trouble!

SEEING Rusty gallop homewards and knowing that he could not possibly catch him, Bernard ran to help Penny who, dazed, was sprawling on the muddy grass.

'Golly!' gasped Bernard, pulling her to her feet. 'I didn't think he'd throw you.' He walked towards the gate, leading Corker. 'Come on. We'd better go and make sure that he's got safely home.'

As they hurried down the road Penny rubbed her aching shoulder.

'Whatever made you do it, Bernard?' Penny asked, puzzled and shaken. 'Why did you rap Rusty's forefeet as he was jumping?'

'Well, it's supposed to be an old horsy dodge,' Bernard explained. 'But I expect it's just one of those ignorant fallacies that know-all horsy types sometimes pass on. It certainly didn't seem to work with Rusty.'

'And I don't think it would do any real good with any pony or horse,' Penny said indignantly.

'Yes, I ought to have known better,' Bernard said sheepishly. 'I am a clot! Sorry, Penny.'

Meanwhile Mr and Mrs Brooke had arrived back at Orchard Cottage from the shop in time to see Rusty, rider-less, with his broken reins trailing and stirrups flying, gallop down the lane and up the path in the dusk.

'Oh dear, *trouble!*' gasped Mrs Brooke, jumping out of the van and, with her husband, running to catch the frightened pony. 'Penny must have been thrown . . . And where's Jane? *Jane . . . !*' she called. 'Where are you?'

Mr Brooke dived to grab Rusty just as the pony swerved away, colliding with Mrs Brooke who, managing to regain her balance, caught Rusty by the cheek-piece of his bridle.

Mr Brooke seized Rusty's trailing reins. 'I'll cope with the pony,' he said. 'Now don't flap, dear. You run down to the field and look for the girls. Give me a shout if you can see either of them.'

'Penny—*Jane!*' Mrs Brooke called, even more worried as the only response was the echo of her own voice.

I mustn't get worked up, Mrs Brooke told herself as she peered frantically through the dusk. I mustn't be the kind of mother who gets into a panic at every pony emergency. But, oh dear, what can have happened to them?

She ran to look in the ditch, and then turned, in anxious surprise, when she heard pony hooves softly thudding on the grass behind her.

'Freckles!' she exclaimed as Jane's grey mare came up to her. Odd! Freckles was not bridled or saddled. So Jane probably had not been riding her. Why?

'Hey, Mummy!'

Relieved to hear Penny's voice, Mrs Brooke ran to the field gate.

'Where are you, darling?' she called through the dusk, and before Penny had a chance to answer she saw her looking over the hedge.

'Mummy! Have you seen Rusty?' Penny asked. 'He bolted.'

'Yes, Daddy's got him now,' said Mrs Brooke. 'But where's Jane?'

'She had to go and play in a hockey match,' Penny explained as they hurried to the yard where Mr Brooke, having removed Rusty's saddle, was rubbing the pony down with a pad of hay to prevent him from catching cold after his wild gallop. 'Were you worried about us, Mummy?' Penny asked.

You'll never realize how much, thought Mrs Brooke, but managed to say quite calmly: 'Well, I did wonder where you and Jane were, dear.'

'Fancy me missing all that excitement to be beaten five-one in a hockey match!' Jane said later that evening. 'I've wanted to meet Bernard Palmer for ages. Everybody says he's got a simply super pony, and to think of all those jumps! Honestly, Penny, you are lucky!'

'I don't know about lucky,' said Penny. 'Rusty's had a dreadful fright—and I think Mummy had a fright, too, when Rusty came galloping home without me. He put his foot through his reins, worst luck, and it will cost at least seven-and-six to have them mended.'

'More pony expense,' sighed Jane. 'There's no end to it.'

Next morning when Jane and Penny went out to the field Freckles and Rusty were grazing. As soon as they head Jane's whistle both ponies lifted their heads and moved towards the girls. Freckles came at her usual smooth trot, but there was something odd about Rusty's action.

'Rusty's going short,' said Penny, watching her pony closely. He was not nodding his head at each step as he would have done if he had been lame in one of his forelegs;

nor was he taking pottering steps as he would if he had been lame in both. 'I think the trouble's in one of his hind legs,' she said as her pony came up for his handful of pony cubes. 'Which is it, boy?'

She rubbed the white star between Rusty's eyes while he lipped up the cubes. When he had eaten the last of them she slipped on his bridle and turned to Jane.

'Watch while I run Rusty up and down,' she said. 'Perhaps you can see on which side he's lame.'

Penny pulled Rusty's reins over his head, and led him down the field at a run.

Jane watched, trying to see how level Rusty carried his hips. Oh dear! So that was it. His left hip was considerably higher than his right. That meant he had strained his left hind leg quite badly, either in the hocks or below.

She looked ruefully at Penny.

'No ride for Rusty today.' She bent to feel Rusty's near hind. 'He's definitely lame. Yes,' she added as she felt a warm and puffy place half-way down the tendon of Rusty's leg. 'It's here. There's heat in it as well as swelling. It's a bad strain.'

'He must have done it galloping home yesterday,' Penny groaned. 'Perhaps he slipped on the cobbles in the village.'

'What bad luck,' sighed Jane, and looked round as she heard pony hooves clip-clopping down the lane.

'Hello!' called Bernard, leaning down from Corker to open the gate. 'I thought I ought to ride over and see how you and Rusty were after the mishap, Penny.'

'I'm all right,' said Penny.

'But Rusty's lame,' added Jane.

Bernard dismounted, and Jane showed him the tender place on Rusty's leg.

'I think it'll need a fomentation, don't you?' she said.

25

Bernard nodded. 'But don't ask me how you do it,' he said, 'because I'm not sure.'

'I am,' said Penny. 'We learned all about it at the Pony Club last month.'

'Oh, yes,' said Jane. 'I remember. The vet told us to warm some kaolin poultice and spread it on grease-proof paper.'

'That's it,' said Penny, 'and you keep it in place with strips of Elastoplast. He said that was better than using a bandage because bandages can sometimes be too loose and cause rubbing—'

'Or sometimes too tight and then they restrict the circulation,' added Jane.

'I wish I'd been here for that lecture,' said Bernard. 'It sounds as if you've got a jolly good Pony Club branch here. I must come to the next rally.'

He walked with the girls towards the garage where the ponies' first-aid kit was kept in a wooden cupboard which Jane had painted white, and on which she had stencilled a blue cross.

'Red Cross for humans—Blue Cross for animals,' said Penny, as Bernard looked at the cupboard, impressed.

'Yes, and the inside bears inspection, too.' Jane opened the cupboard door. 'We restocked it only last week. Of course the ideal way is to replace any of the contents as soon as they're used up, and that's what we intend to do in future.'

Bernard peered inside, touching various bottles, tins and packages. 'Iodine for cuts and scratches,' he noticed. 'Salt for washing wounds; Acriflavine cream for putting on after-wards; a thermometer; blunt-ended scissors—'

'Those are for cutting the hair away from a wound,' explained Penny.

'And here's some cotton-wool.' Jane showed Bernard. 'We put it in this sponge-bag to keep it clean.'

'We've got a sponge, too, and some soap,' Penny said, 'and here's the kaolin poultice.' She lifted out the tin.

'I see you've got plenty of Elastoplast, too,' said Bernard.

Jane nodded. 'We've got a roll of inch-wide waterproof Elastoplast,' she said, 'and a two-and-a-half-inch-wide Elastoplast bandage so that we can cut off what we need.'

'I'd never have believed it,' Bernard said, gazing at the first-aid cupboard in admiration. 'It's almost too good to be true. I haven't got half these things in my tack room. But—' he added, a twinkle in his brown eyes, 'I have got a few other essential things that you don't seem to have here.'

'Have you?' asked Jane. 'What?'

'A bottle of horse-embrocation,' Bernard ticked off the items on his fingers. 'Lead lotion to put on strains and bruises after you've got rid of the inflammation, and a tin of sulphur ointment for cracked heels.' He broke off. 'Oh, and I've got two or three cough drinks, and a couple of colic drinks just in case.'

'I suppose the cough drinks are all right,' said Jane. 'But I'm not sure about the colic drinks. The Pony Club vet said that if a pony gets colic one ought to put on a rug to keep it warm, walk it about to stop it lying down and send for the vet right away. He said that colic can be too serious for young people to treat without skilled advice.'

'Fair enough,' said Bernard and cocked his head to listen to a plaintive whinny from the field. 'Meanwhile our pony-patient awaits his treatment. Come on!'

FOUR

Rusty refuses

JANE and Penny poulticed Rusty's strain every three hours, taking care not to get the kaolin too hot because they knew that a pony's skin was very sensitive, and that Rusty could not bear the dressing applied as hot as could a human being.

They alternated the treatment with running a trickle of cold water from the garden-hose, being careful to play the hose first on Rusty's foot to accustom him to it before moving the trickle up to the tender area of the strain.

It was not until the following Thursday that Rusty's lameness had quite gone, and the girls decided that Penny might ride him again.

Thursday was half-day closing in Easthampton and Mr Brooke was at home that afternoon, so when Jane and Penny came back from school he went out with them to catch the ponies.

'Mr Shaw from the riding school came into the shop this morning,' he told the girls. 'He wanted to buy a battery for the tack-room transistor. He was asking how you were getting on, so I told him that Rusty has been lame, but that I thought he seemed better, and you were going to take him out today.'

'Did Mr Shaw think it would be all right to ride him?' Penny asked.

Mr Brooke nodded. 'So long as you're careful,' he said. 'Mr Shaw made the point that you mustn't take him on any uneven ground or in any heavy going, and he said no cantering or galloping. Steady walking on a level surface is what Rusty needs now.'

Penny found that Mr Shaw's advice was sound. Rusty's lameness did not return and on Friday Penny took him a little farther and did some trotting as well as walking. By Saturday he was cantering and, on Sunday, Penny felt it was safe to jump him again.

In the morning Jane and Penny had to go to church with their mother, but, after lunch, they were allowed to ride. Bernard arrived on Corker and they saddled up. First, they put a single cavalletti, eighteen inches high, in the middle of the field. Bernard popped Corker over and Jane followed on Freckles. Then it was the turn of Rusty who had been tossing his head with seeming impatience.

'Right you are, boy. Off you go!' Penny leaned forward in her saddle and touched the chestnut pony with her heels.

Instead of eagerly setting off towards the obstacle as Penny had anticipated, Rusty cantered 'on the spot' and then danced sideways. A tell-tale froth appeared at the butt of his snaffle.

'Come on, Rusty,' Penny encouraged, stroking his neck. 'There's nothing to get worked up about. You can easily jump this.'

She gave him a determined jab with her heels, and rode him at the cavalletti. When he was a couple of strides away from the jump Rusty stopped, and stood trembling. Cold sweat was already beginning to break out on his neck and flanks.

'Jane! Bernard!' Penny called. 'Rusty doesn't want to jump. He seems scared.'

Bernard trotted up. 'I suppose he remembers the tap that

I was idiot enough to give him last time he jumped,' he said regretfully. 'What do we do now?'

'Try coaxing him,' suggested Jane. 'Wait a minute—' She dismounted, and handed her reins to Bernard. 'Hold Freckles for me . . . I've got an idea.'

Bernard and Penny watched while Jane ran towards the cottage. Soon she was back again, carrying Rusty's wooden feeding box.

'What's in there?' Penny called while Rusty turned his head inquiringly and sniffed.

'That's what Rusty would like to know,' said Jane, placing the box on the ground on the far side of the jump. 'There you are, Rusty!' she called. 'You'll have to take the jump if you want to find out what's in here.'

Rusty's ears pricked. His nostrils widened. On the breeze he could sniff the tantalizing smell of pony cubes and molasses—a pony treat.

'Go on, Rusty.' Penny's legs and hands drove him at the jump.

As Penny leaned forward, the pony still hesitated, torn

30

between fear of the jump and longing for the sweet molasses. Penny urged him on with her heels. Rusty could resist the temptation no longer. Still nervously eyeing the cavalletti, he increased his pace. Penny kept him straight at the jump. Her heels drove him on at every stride. One-two-three-*up!* Rusty jumped high. He was not going to risk touching the cavalletti in case he got hit again. Once safely on the other side he stretched out his neck and raced for the molasses.

'Don't let him eat it all,' Jane warned, running to take the feeding box when Rusty had eaten just enough of the cubes and molasses to whet his appetite for more.

Meanwhile Bernard had put another cavalletti on top of the one in the middle of the field, and placed a second one in front of them, making a higher, sloping jump.

'Try that, Penny,' he called, scrambling on to Corker's back. 'Wait a minute. I'll give you a lead.'

Penny could barely hold Rusty in check until Bernard and Corker were clear. Rusty was only too eager to get over the jump and reach his reward—the molasses and pony cubes that Jane was now placing on the other side.

Penny shortened her reins as Rusty cantered up to the jump. This time Rusty jumped bigger than ever—and Penny, left behind, found herself strap-hanging on the reins to keep her balance. On landing, Rusty snatched at his bit, stuck out his nose and galloped to the feeding bucket.

They did not have any more trouble getting Rusty to jump. The problem now was that he jumped too big and raced on after landing even though Penny and Jane had discontinued his titbits.

Being only twelve, and not having very long legs or well-developed riding muscles, Penny often found it difficult to keep her seat. Try as she might, she could not help riding by a mixture of balance and holding-on by the reins. As was to be expected, this made Rusty inclined to toss his head and pull.

All the same, Jane and Penny were pleased with the progress that Rusty had made. Freckles, too, had benefited from the well-planned and progressively more difficult jumping-training. A good and steady natural jumper, she was now acquiring flexibility and balance.

Bernard and Corker often came to Orchard Cottage to ride with the girls, and the three of them devised various jump-combinations with the cavalletti, building them sometimes into a triple-bar, sometimes into parallel bars, or in-and-outs, and altering the distances between the jumps so as to vary the number of strides that the ponies had to take between obstacles. All this was intended to make the ponies handy; or to give them control over their movements, and to make them 'think', so that they would be able to tackle any 'trappy' and unusual obstacles which they might meet.

A week before the beginning of the Easter holidays Jane came down to breakfast to find a postcard by her plate. It was addressed to the Misses Jane and Penelope Brooke, and on turning it over she saw, in the top right-hand corner, the Pony Club badge.

Penny, too, caught sight of it as she carried in the milk and breakfast flakes from the kitchen.

'What's that?' she asked, craning over Jane's shoulder, and only just missing spilling some of the milk down Jane's neck.

'*A mounted rally*,' Jane read out, '*will be held at Moss Green Stables at 2 p.m. on Wednesday, April the 10th. There will be instruction, jumping practice, and an opportunity to take the tests.*'

'Gosh!' said Penny, delighted. 'That sounds simply super!'

'Doesn't it?' Jane looked up. 'Now we'll be able to take our Standard C.'

Penny put the packet of flakes and the milk jug on the table and went to the writing desk. 'Where's the test card?' she asked, rummaging through the contents. 'I want to see what we've got to do.'

'And I want to see you eat up your breakfast and catch the bus to school,' put in Mrs Brooke, coming through the doorway with a dish of sausages and bacon. 'Come on now. Hurry up!'

Penny ate her breakfast and after putting on her hat and coat went back into the sitting-room to look for the Pony Club test card before setting off for the bus. She had to run all the way down the lane, and arrived at the cross-roads panting and with her shoe-lace undone just as the bus was drawing up.

'Penny!' Jane sighed, putting up a hand to straighten Penny's beret in elder-sisterly impatience. 'You do look a sight! And whatever have you been doing? Honestly, you are the end. You get later and later. You'll miss the bus altogether one of these days, and then Miss Tate will create.'

'Oh, pipe down, Jane,' Penny said, unconcerned as she followed her sister up the steps to the top deck. 'You won't grumble at me when you see what I've got.' She produced the green Pony Club test card. 'Come on. Let's sit by ourselves and then we can see what we shall have to do to pass.'

Together Jane and Penny pored over the printed card.

'*Standard C*,' read Jane. '*Riding. Should have a seat independent of the reins and be able to maintain the correct seat and position of the hands. Have control of the pony, with a knowledge of the correct aids in elementary movements, i.e. turn on the move, circles, increase and decrease of pace.*' Jane's voice rose in excitement. '*Be able to jump low fences.*'

'We can do that all right,' Penny said confidently.

'*Stable Management*,' went on Jane. '*Know the essential grooming kit and its uses. Be capable of saddling, bridling and rugging-up. Have an elementary understanding of the care and cleaning of saddlery. Have an elementary understanding of feeding, watering and cleanliness of the horse. Have a knowledge of the care and working of a pony off grass. Recognize a loose or worn shoe, risen clench, excessively long foot and know what action to take. Know the points of a horse.*'

'We know most of the stable management,' nodded Penny, 'because we have to look after Rusty and Freckles. But what about the points of a horse? There are such a lot,' she added, thoughtfully. 'I'm not very sure of those.'

FIVE

Penny is ashamed

DURING the first four days of the Easter holidays Jane, Penny and Bernard schooled their ponies for the Pony Club test. They practised moving off correctly from a walk and changing smoothly to a trot and to a canter, back to a trot and halting properly—not just by hauling on the reins, but by a gentle pull and conveying their wishes to their ponies by leaning slightly back, throwing their weight down into the saddle and putting the lower parts of their legs against the ponies' girths.

They knew that to make their ponies walk or trot they should close both legs to their ponies' sides, and ease both reins slightly. To canter, they 'collected' their ponies with a 'feel' on the reins, sat down in their saddles, gripped with their thighs and knees, and gave their ponies a touch with their heels.

Rusty had difficulty in reining back. Freckles and Corker did this easily, but at first Rusty did not seem to know what Penny wanted him to do. She closed both legs hard against Rusty's sides and turned in her wrists 'feeling' his mouth slightly harder to make him step back. But Rusty just looked puzzled and shook his head against the pressure of the bit. So Jane stood beside him facing his tail, and put her hand on his bridle by the bit. As Penny took a 'feel' on the reins, Jane stepped forward, making Rusty step back. So, one step at a time, they taught the colt how to rein back.

'That only leaves the points of a horse,' Penny said two

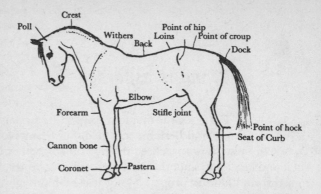

nights before the Pony Club rally, getting down one of her pony books from the shelf, and poring over the illustration of a pony with his points marked by arrows.

'Ear, poll, crest, mane, withers, back, loins, point of hip, point of croup . . . Oh, dear,' she groaned. 'It really is quite hard.'

'Yes, but think how much more interesting than learning French verbs,' consoled Jane.

By the afternoon of the Pony Club rally, Penny had mastered the points of the horse and was feeling quite confident when, after an early lunch, she and Jane set off to call for Bernard so that they could all ride together to Moss Green Stables, where the rally was to be held.

The rally was fun. It took place in a large field behind the Moss Green riding stables, most of the pupils of which were there on the school's ponies. There was an assortment of riders, aged from as young as two years old to about seventeen. The youngest child of all was mounted in a basket-chair saddle on a donkey. There were two four-year-old

twins—a boy and a girl—on very small Exmoor ponies. A
boy, a little older, was riding a mischievous black Shetland,
and there were children of all sizes on Dartmoor, Exmoor,
and Welsh ponies and cobs, 'blood' ponies, a hairy-heeled
Fell pony, a beautiful grey Highland mare, full of bone and
up to any weight, with a sweet and gentle expression, an
Anglo-Arab, a Norwegian, and several that were just
'pony'.

As soon as everybody had arrived Major Kirkwood, the
District Commissioner, called all the members into a circle
and gave a brief and interesting talk on the care of a pony at
grass. He emphasized how important it was to make sure
that there was always fresh, clean water in the field, and that
the pony had a salt-lick to provide the essential minerals
that he needed.

'Many ponies are not kept as well as they might be,'
Major Kirkwood told the listening Pony Club members.
'This is not due to wilful neglect or lack of feeling on the part
of their owners. It is usually due to ignorance, and "not
liking to ask" for information and advice.'

He glanced round at them all from under his bushy eyebrows.

'You Pony Club youngsters are lucky because you have
your lecturers and officials to ask, and, I hope—' his keen
glance swept round them all—'that none of you will be
afraid to ask about anything that puzzles you.

'I expect all of you know that your ponies need feeding
during the winter months even though they are out at grass,
but how many of you realize that, during the summer holidays when you are riding them nearly every day, and they're
out of their fields for long hours at a time, they don't get
much chance to graze, and so they need a short feed—about
a couple of pounds—of pony cubes, or some oats, mixed

with a double handful of chaff or bran to make them eat slowly and chew well?'

A tall fair-haired boy of about fifteen broke in to ask a question: 'Should our ponies be having short feeds now, sir?'

'Certainly they should,' Major Kirkwood told him. 'This is the time of the year—at the start of the Easter holidays—when a pony's condition is at its lowest. Over the winter he has used up all his surplus fat. He's about to change his coat, and the grass hasn't really started to grow. So, you see, Derek,'—he smiled at the boy—'your pony should still be on his winter rations; he should be having his hay-net filled every morning and being given another netful of hay with a short feed, such as I have described, in the afternoon. In winter you should spread out his feeds over the day. In that way he gets the maximum warmth, benefit and interest from them.'

'When should a pony be put on winter rations?' a girl wanted to know, and the Major replied that so long as a pony was having a short feed daily and the grazing was good, there was no need to start giving him additional hay until November.

'The only two months of the year when there is really absolutely no need to supplement the natural grass,' he went on, 'are May and June when the grazing has its full feed value.'

Penny and Jane thought the talk was very interesting and, as Bernard summed it up—'Just what everybody wanted to know and not too much for us to remember.'

Afterwards the rally divided into 'rides', some to take the various tests, and others for instruction, according to the standards of their horsemanship. Penny, Jane and Bernard, with five other children, went to Mrs Irvine who was going to examine them in the stable-management part of their Standard C test.

They were the first three to be examined, and Mrs Irvine said that they obviously looked after their own ponies well and had a good knowledge of the subject.

'That means we've passed,' Penny whispered to Jane as they led their ponies into the next paddock where Major Kirkwood was going to test their riding ability. He told Penny, Jane, Bernard and a girl called Felicity Macgregor, who had followed them across from Mrs Irvine's group, to mount and to proceed round the paddock at a walk. He watched them all keenly as he gave the order to trot, and then to canter.

After a short gallop he halted them and called them to the middle in turn to ride individual circles. Then, they all moved into another field where a series of low jumps were set up. At one end of the field the more advanced riders, who had already passed Standard C, were schooling over

more difficult jumps with Madge Stevens—the girl who had helped Jane and Penny to break-in Rusty, and who now had her own riding-school.

Rusty watched the other ponies with interest while Bernard and Corker cantered up to the first of the four small, brushwood fences that Major Kirkwood had asked them to jump.

Major Kirkwood made Bernard jump the course twice. Then he said that he was satisfied with his standard of riding and that Bernard could join the more advanced riders who were jumping at the other end of the field.

Jane was the next to jump and Rusty impatiently shifted his feet while she and Freckles had their turn. Freckles, as always, took the obstacles easily and steadily and Major Kirkwood was very pleased.

'Splendid!' he told Jane when she had finished. 'Your pony jumps well and you have a strong independent seat. You sit well forward, putting no weight on your pony's loins, and letting your wrists 'give' when she jumps so as not to interfere with her mouth. I'm very pleased with you. So off you go to join the advanced group . . . Next please!'

As Jane rode off Penny trotted Rusty forward. The chestnut pony's ears pricked and he cantered keenly towards the jumps. Rusty now liked jumping. He knew that there was sometimes a titbit when he got to the other side. Penny and Jane had not always rewarded him, but sometimes they had done, and Rusty lived in hope. This made him take his fences rather fast.

Also at the back of his pony mind still lingered the memory of the rap that Bernard had given him to make him pick up his feet, and so he still jumped higher than was necessary. In fact Rusty jumped very big, and, as usual, Penny was apt to be unbalanced. She did not realize this, nor that she was using her reins to keep her seat. Rusty cleared all the jumps and Penny felt that she had done rather well. She cantered back to Major Kirkwood.

'Shall I go and join the others?' she asked with a bright smile.

Major Kirkwood did not smile back. Instead he looked sorry. 'I don't like to disappoint you,' he said in a kindly voice, 'particularly after your sister's done so well . . .'

Penny's smile faded. 'But Rusty's cleared all the fences—' she began.

'That's not the point.' From under his bushy eyebrows, Major Kirkwood's steel-blue eyes looked straight at Penny. 'The Pony Club doesn't just expect you to get over the jumps,' he explained gently; 'it wants you to make it pleasant for your pony while you're clearing them.'

Penny was dismayed.

'When you jump,' Major Kirkwood went on, 'you're apt to keep your balance by hanging on to Rusty's reins. That can't be very comfortable for him, and, if you keep it up, you may "spoil his mouth" and make him into an obstinate pony. You're inclined to "strap-hang", too, when you're trotting and cantering.' He paused and gave Penny an understanding smile. 'Now don't be too down-hearted. It's not easy, I know. Your pony is young and high-spirited, and it isn't your fault that your legs aren't yet long enough, nor your muscles developed enough, for you to have a really strong seat. But you can improve, you know.' He nodded his head towards the other group where Jane was now taking her turn to put Freckles over a three-foot gate. 'Get that sister of yours to put you on the lunging-rein. You need practice in riding without reins, arms folded and stirrups crossed. Circle first at a walk and a trot and then jump some cavalletti or quite low poles still without reins and stirrups.'

'I'll do that,' Penny promised in a small voice, feeling quite ashamed.

'Cheer up!' Major Kirkwood smiled encouragingly at her. 'There'll be another working rally before the end of the Easter holidays, so you'll be able to try the test again.'

Penny was still feeling subdued when, at the end of the rally, she set off with Jane and Bernard to ride home. Jane and Bernard, however, were so full of the afternoon's happenings that they did not even notice that Penny was unusually quiet.

'We've had a wonderful time,' Jane told her sister. 'Madge Stevens said that Corker had the makings of a really good jumper. She was pleased with Freckles, too— and do you know what?—Bernard and I have been picked to train with the team for the inter-branch Pony Club competitions! Isn't it simply terrific?'

SIX

Disaster on the moors

'YOU'VE been quiet all evening,' Jane said to Penny when they were going to bed that night. 'Whatever's the matter with you? I hope you're not sickening for anything.'

Under the bedroom light she scrutinized her young sister's face. 'No spots—thank goodness! It'd be dreadful if you got measles or something—and we were both put into quarantine, just when I've got the chance of getting into the Pony Club team.'

Penny's lip trembled. She could not hide her disappointment any longer, so she turned away from Jane and, pulling back the curtains, looked forlornly across the moonlit garden to the field where she could see Freckles' grey shape and Rusty's darker outline, nose to tail, heads down, dozing under the lee of the hedge.

I've let you down, Rusty, she thought. There I was—believing that I was making a really good jumper of you, and all the time I have been hurting your mouth, dragging on your reins and spoiling you. And I didn't know. I wouldn't have hurt you for anything.

'Penny!' Jane's exasperated voice broke into her younger sister's dejection. 'Talking to you is like talking to a brick wall. What are you sulking about? Are you jealous because Bernard and I have been picked for the team?'

Penny couldn't answer. Tears were trickling down her face.

'Oh, cry baby!' Jane walked to the door. She felt grown-up and quite impatient. 'I'm not going to waste my time talking to you if you can't pull yourself together.'

In the bathroom Jane brushed her teeth more vigorously than usual. She was feeling guilty now. Obviously Penny's day had been disappointing. She hadn't passed the test at the Pony Club Rally, and perhaps Major Kirkwood had been critical. Poor Penny! Jane could imagine how she felt. No wonder she had burst into tears.

Jane rinsed her toothbrush under the tap, put it into its holder, and hurried back to Penny to make amends.

'I'm sorry, Penny—' she began, and then stopped. Far from her sister being in tears, she was sitting on the bed, intently reading a pony book.

'What did you say, Jane?' Penny's finger marked the passage that she had been reading. 'It seems I've been going too fast with Rusty. I've been trying to make him into a jumper before I've made myself into a really good rider. I've got to go back a bit, and I shall need your help.'

'Good for you,' said Jane. 'You can count on me.'

She listened as Penny outlined her plan, and the two girls were still talking half an hour after they had put out the light.

Next morning, Penny got out the lunge-rein and buckled it to the ring which had been fitted to the noseband of Rusty's bridle when he was being broken in. She saddled the pony, put on a pair of side-reins which she fastened through his girths, being careful to adjust them to allow Rusty to move with a stride of normal length but, at the same time, preventing him from turning his head to either side or unduly increasing the length of his stride.

'Don't forget to put this round his neck.' Jane handed her an old stirrup-leather to use as a neck-strap. 'If you want to grab at something you can grab at that instead of the reins and then you won't jab Rusty in the mouth.'

Penny buckled the strap round Rusty's neck.

'Up you go!' Jane held the colt's head while Penny mounted.

They moved into the middle of the field, and then Penny knotted her reins and crossed her stirrups. She tried to sit in a relaxed way with her legs hanging loosely down and her hands resting on her thighs. Then she put her hands through Rusty's neck-strap and brought her knees slightly forward until they were lightly gripping the saddle behind the knee rolls.

Jane straightened Penny's leg so that it hung down vertically from the knee and moved her foot into position so that her toes were slightly higher than her heels.

Penny sat well down in the saddle and, feeling secure, let go of the neck-strap.

'Put your hands on your hips,' said Jane. 'Fold them

behind your back. Now stretch them out in front of you and then swing them sideways. Again!'

Penny repeated the suppling and balancing exercises while Rusty stood quite still. His right ear kept flicking back in a puzzled way, but he was not at all restless. During his training Penny and Jane had tapped his hooves with hammers, coughed loudly near him, opened umbrellas, blown whistles and done everything they could think of to accustom him to odd happenings. So what they were doing now did not upset him in the least.

'Arms upward stretch,' Jane told Penny. 'Now down. Now up again!'

Penny laughed. 'You sound just like Miss Yates at school,' she said. 'P.T. on ponies! I wonder what she'd say about that?'

Penny's next exercise was trunk-turning from side to side with her hands on her hips. Then Jane told her to put her hands through the neck-strap and she began to lunge Rusty in a circle at a walk.

At first Penny felt strange, riding on a saddle but without stirrups and reins. The saddle felt much more slippery than riding on Rusty's bare back would have done, but she soon got used to it and was confident enough to let go of the neck-strap. After five or six circles, Jane shook the lunge-rein and urged Rusty to a trot.

'That's good, Penny,' she called encouragingly. 'No, don't let your legs swing! They're moving in time with Rusty. Keep them still. Sit up straight. You're dropping your inside leg and leaning inward . . . That's better.'

Penny tried hard to correct her faults. Jane stopped Rusty and made him circle in the other direction, first at a walk and then at a trot.

'I think that's enough for today,' Jane decided after about a quarter of an hour. 'Rusty's beginning to get bored.'

She called Rusty to her and unbuckled the lunge-rein.

'What now?' Penny asked.

'Let's go for a ride,' suggested Jane.

While Penny trotted Rusty round the paddock practising circles on either rein, Jane brushed the overnight mud from Freckles, picked out her feet, and put on her saddle and bridle. Then, side by side, the two girls set off down the lane and headed towards Whinberry Common.

As soon as Rusty felt the short turf under his feet he was keen to canter. Freckles, too, seemed eager, so Jane and Penny gave them their heads, and settled down to enjoy the thrill of a gallop. With the ponies' hooves sending up bits of muddy turf, they sped past the gorse bushes and the pond. It was not until they breasted the sharp rise of Rowan Hill, where the green croziers of the young bracken were pushing through the turf, that the ponies' thudding hooves slowed. They reached the top and pulled up for a breather. Then they set off again at a walk along the narrow track of Windy

Ridge, and turned down the steep path to Bluebell Hollow. The ponies picked their way carefully down the loose pebbly surface.

Jane and Penny leant slightly back and put their weight into their stirrups to steady the ponies. When they got to the bottom they rode along the sandy lane besides the stream and Penny practised riding without rising to the trot in order to get her seat lower in the saddle and so more secure.

'Put your hands through the neck-strap,' advised Jane, 'in case you find yourself tempted to keep your balance by hanging on to the reins.'

When they again slowed to a walk Penny took her feet out of the stirrups, and tried to sit as far down in the saddle as she could.

'That's a good idea,' Jane approved, doing the same. 'It's all a matter of practice and being aware of one's bad riding habits and trying to cure them. On the other hand, I suppose we don't want to become so conscious of our faults that we ride stiffly. I expect the answer is to try to achieve a firm, but natural, seat independent of the reins.'

Walking and trotting they rode through the valley. Rusty and Freckles were looking alertly about them and obviously enjoying the outing.

They forded the stream by the footbridge and climbed the heather-clad slope on the other side. Below them an unfenced road with a peaty gully on either side crossed the moor. There were sheep grazing below and, as Penny and Jane watched, one of them wandered on to the road and stood suckling her lamb. As the lamb fed, its tail jerked ecstatically.

'What a sweet little lamb,' said Penny.

'All white and woolly,' said Jane. 'And isn't its mother proud?'

'Oh, goodness!' Penny gasped when, from round a rocky outcrop came a car, pulling a horse-trailer. 'Look out!' she shouted as the driver, unseeing, swept straight at the lamb and its mother.

There was a screech of brakes. The sheep and lamb skittered into the heather while the car, hitting a greasy patch, skidded. The horse-trailer swung with it. The coupling bar snapped. The trailer landed in the gully half-tilted; one wheel in the air still turning.

'Oh, how dreadful!' Jane's hands tightened on her reins. 'There may be a horse in there—' Even before she had

finished speaking a frightened squeal came from the inside of the trailer, followed by crashes and thuds as the panic-stricken horse tried to kick its way out.

'It'll hurt itself,' gasped Penny.

'Come on,' urged Jane.

Jane jumped off Freckles' back and, pulling her reins over the pony's head, plunged down the hillside followed by Penny.

Stumbling over tufts of heather and with the tough stems of last year's dead bracken catching round their ankles, they ran to the scene of the accident.

Squeals and kicks were still coming from the ditched trailer, and, from the car, a fair-haired girl was staggering, a hand to her head as though she were dazed. Then, with an effort, she seemed to pull herself together, ran to the back of the trailer, and tugged at the bolt that held the ramp.

'Do you want any help?' Jane panted.

'Yes—quickly!' The girl sounded frantic. 'The bolt's jammed and we've got to get this trailer open somehow. Gay Fella's hurt. Look!'

Jane and Penny gazed in dismay at the patch of blood that was seeping from the trailer.

SEVEN

Jump to it!

'WE'VE got to get Gay Fella out,' the girl gasped. Desperately she glanced around and, picking up a stone, hammered at the bolt. 'Oh, heavens! That's jammed it even more. What can we do?'

'A tool kit!' Jane suggested. 'Have you got one in the car?'

'Yes, I'll fetch it.'

The girl ran to the boot and suddenly Gay Fella's squealing stopped, while Freckles, having scented blood, was backing uneasily away.

Jane looked at Penny in despair. 'This is dreadful,' she said. 'To think that this should happen to Gay Fella. We've seen his pictures. He jumps at all the big shows—'

She broke off as the girl hurried back, unrolling the tool kit and grabbing a tyre-lever.

She tried to force back the bolt but it would not move. Meanwhile Jane was searching among the tools.

'Here! Let's try this.'

Jane picked up a screwdriver, and began to turn one of the two screws that held the bolt-socket.

'That's clever,' the fair-haired girl said gratefully. 'I'd never have thought of that.'

Now Jane was getting out the second screw, and, though her haste made her fumble, at last it dropped to the ground, and the bolt was free.

In the tilted van Gay Fella was leaning against the wall,

unable to stand upright. His eyes were glazed, and scarlet blood was spurting rhythmically—a dread sign of arterial bleeding—from a deep gash in his off-fore. They must act quickly. Gay Fella had already lost a lot of blood, and was in danger of bleeding to death.

Jane and Penny knew what the girl was going to do when  she hurriedly unknotted her tie.

'Yes, that's right,' said Jane. 'A tourniquet. Here!' She held out her switch. The fair-haired girl climbed into the trailer and crouched to wind her tie round Gay Fella's leg above the wound. She fastened it tightly, and made a loop against the knot through which she thrust Penny's switch, twisting it to tighten the tie, and so stop the bleeding by cutting off the circulation of blood to the wound.

'We must get a vet,' she told Jane and Penny. 'I've got to stay here with Gay Fella to loosen the tourniquet every twenty minutes. If his circulation is cut off for longer than that, gangrene might set in. Will one of you ride to a telephone?'

'I'll go.' Jane's foot was already in Freckles' stirrup. She flung herself into the saddle and urged the ever-willing Freckles into a fast canter along the heathery verge of the road.

But where was the nearest telephone? The only box was on Hamley Green three miles away. Jane glanced at the line of telephone poles stretching into the distance. She rode on, watching the poles. Sooner or later she knew she would see a pair of wires branching off to a farm or cottage. Yes, there they were, leading over the fields to a grey stone farm, a quarter of a mile away on the brow of a hill. But there seemed to be no way to the farm. The lane must be on the other side of the hill.

Well, she would have to go across country. Cramming down her cap and sitting forward, Jane turned Freckles and rode her at the hedge. With a lurch, Freckles heaved herself over, stumbled on landing, recovered and set off again while Jane, thrown on to her neck, struggled back into the saddle.

The field was ploughed and the going was heavy. Mud spattered Jane as Freckles galloped across the furrows. On the other side was a fence with barbed wire. Jane's heart sank. Then she saw a stile at the corner of the field. The stile looked solid and high—a difficult jump, but it was better than risking the barbed wire. Freckles seemed to sense her rider's urgency, and, as Jane touched her with her heels, calling for greater speed to carry them over the obstacle, Freckles stretched out her neck and responded gallantly.

The grey mare cleared the stile with half a foot to spare and galloped up the hill to the farm. At the farmyard gate Jane jumped off, and, lifting, pushed the gate over the rutted earth, wide enough to lead Freckles through.

The farmer's wife looked startled when Jane, muddy and flushed, ran into the farmyard with Freckles.

'Oh, dear! What is it, love?' the woman asked, wiping her hands on her apron as she came to the door. 'Has there been an accident? Is somebody hurt?'

'Not somebody—it's a horse,' Jane explained breathlessly while she tied up Freckles. 'It's Gay Fella—you know, the show jumper—David Leslie's horse.'

'And you need help!' exclaimed the woman. 'I'll come, but my husband and all the men are out.'

'Never mind,' said Jane. 'Just let me use your telephone. I must get the vet quickly. Gay Fella's bleeding from an artery. There's a girl with him—his groom, I suppose. She's put on a tourniquet, but it would be dangerous to leave it on for very long.'

'Come in, love. The telephone's through here.' The woman flung open an inner door. 'Do you know the number?'

'By heart!' Jane thought feelingly as she dialled the vet's number—Easthampton 431.

'That should do it.' Mr Marsh, the vet, straightened up after bandaging Gay Fella's leg. He put away the surgical silk and needle in his instrument case and took out a hypodermic syringe. 'I'll give him an anti-tetanus injection,' he said, 'just to be sure.'

'Better to be sure than sorry,' Ann Taylor, Gay Fella's girl groom said fervently, 'especially when you're dealing with a thousand pounds' worth of horse. Mr Leslie's abroad, but goodness knows what he'll say when he gets back and hears about this mishap!'

'He's in Spain, isn't he?' Penny's eyes widened with excitement. 'Jumping in the international competitions.' She looked up at Ann. 'Why didn't he take Gay Fella?'

'Gay Fella's been having a rest,' the fair-haired girl explained. 'Mr Leslie will be jumping him later in the season. He's taken Blue Boy and Toscanini to Spain.'

The injured horse shifted his feet restlessly on the short grass at the roadside, and she patted him reassuringly.

'As a matter of fact I've just been to fetch Gay Fella from Green Meadows where he's been wintering,' she went on. 'He's been out at grass as you can see by his coat. I'm taking him home to get him ready for the British shows.'

'We knew Mr Leslie lived near here,' said Jane, 'but we never thought we'd meet his horse.'

'It's a good thing for Gay Fella that you did,' Ann said warmly. 'I don't know what I'd have done without your help.'

By now Mr Marsh was getting into his car. 'I'll call at Spencer's Garage on the way back, and get them to bring a breakdown-lorry to get your trailer out of the ditch. Then you'll be able to put Gay Fella in, and they'll tow him home I don't want him to walk much until his leg's healed.'

'I wonder how Gay Fella's getting on,' Penny said next morning, as she and Jane were saddling and bridling Rusty and fitting on his side-reins and lunge. 'I wish we knew.'

'So do I,' said Jane. 'Did you notice the little lucky "star" on his forehead? It's too small to show up in the photographs.'

'Yes, wasn't he wonderful?' Penny's tone was awed. 'And

wasn't he *big?* He must have been nearly seventeen hands. Fancy a girl like Ann Taylor being able to take complete charge of him. I do think she's lucky being groom to a famous show jumper.'

'Better than having to slave for the G.C.E.,' Jane sighed. 'But I suppose she's got hers, *and* her Pony Club Standard A, too. A girl doesn't get a super job like that unless she's worked jolly hard for it.'

Rusty bunted Penny in the middle of her back to remind them of his presence, and Penny mounted, crossing her stirrups, while Jane, at the other end of the lunge-rein, took charge. Penny repeated the exercises of the previous day. Then Jane lunged Rusty and Penny rode, still without stirrups or reins, several circles in either direction at the walk and at the trot.

Next she carried out suppling exercises while on the move, riding with her arms folded behind her back, and then doing arm-swinging up and down.

After several such practices, Penny, instead of feeling precarious and being jolted about, was developing a strong seat.

On the next Wednesday evening Bernard telephoned to tell Jane that there was to be a jumping practice for the Pony Club team on the following day.

'I'll be away all day,' Jane told her family when she came back into the sitting-room, eyes shining. 'So I'll need sandwiches, Mummy.'

'What exactly's happening?' Mr Brooke lowered his *Television Dealers' Gazette.*

Jane explained. '—And you see, Daddy, the practice is being held at Madge Stevens' stables. They're about six miles away. There'll be jumping in the morning and the afternoon, so I shan't be able to come back to lunch.'

Mr Brooke put his hand in his pocket for his pipe, and then remembered that he had given up smoking when his daughters had started to keep a pony. 'Jumping practice, eh?' he echoed. 'What's all this leading up to?'

'Well, I'm in the team for the Inter-Branch Pony Club Competitions,' Jane said. 'Good, isn't it?'

'Is it?' Mr Brooke blinked. 'This all seems a lot more ambitious than the bit of jumping in the field that I said you could do, doesn't it?'

'Well, perhaps,' said Jane, 'but they need me. You see, quite a few of the Pony Club members go to boarding school; so they're not at home to take part in the practices during term-time. That's why the committee have decided to build up a team of the boys and girls who go to day-schools, so that they and their ponies will be in good trim for the competitions in the summer holidays.'

'I see,' her father said doubtfully. 'But how much is all this going to cost? Are there going to be a lot of horse-box expenses, moving the ponies over half the country?'

'There shouldn't be,' said Jane. 'Of course the finals will be held away, but the first heats will be jumped off among the nearest branches. It's unlikely that our branch will be in the finals, and, if we were, perhaps I'd be able to earn the transport money in some way or another. Lots of girls take part-time jobs in the summer holidays.'

'Let's meet that when we come to it, dear,' said Mrs Brooke, putting her mending into her work basket. She looked across at her husband. 'It seems harmless enough to me, George, and I think it's nice for Jane and Penny to make friends with other pony children as they have done at the Pony Club.' She stood up as though the discussion was ended. 'I'm going to make us all a drink of cocoa before the girls go to bed.'

'Jane's having a lot of fun at the Pony Club,' Penny said to her mother next morning after her sister had ridden away. 'But it's not much fun for me. I'm not in the team, and I'm not likely to be in it because, even if I got to jump well enough before the summer holidays, Rusty's too young and temperamental to be trusted to jump with other ponies in pairs and threes as they'll probably be doing in the competition. And now Jane's going to be away at these practices and I haven't even got anyone to lunge Rusty. I'll never pass Standard C.'

Mrs Brooke put the last cup on to its hook on the kitchen dresser and looked at the clock. 'Daddy's having his lunch in town today, and Jane won't be coming back, so there's only you and me, Penny, and if you don't mind having baked beans on toast and a piece of cake for lunch I needn't cook. Then I'll have time to help you with Rusty.'

Penny cheered up. 'Oh, Mummy, that would be super.'

So Mrs Brooke took over the lunge-rein and put Penny and Rusty through their paces. As Penny had expected, Jane was away quite a lot during the Easter holidays, training with the Pony Club team, and so Mrs Brooke took her elder daughter's place in lunging Rusty. Penny soon advanced to jumping the cavalletti on the lunge and also to riding Rusty down the jumping lane. For both these exercises it was necessary to remove the side reins so as to give Rusty free movement of his head. At the next working rally, in the last week of the holidays, Penny entered again for the riding part of the Standard C test.

This time she passed.

'You've improved a lot, Penny,' Major Kirkwood told her with a delighted smile. 'Well done!'

Triumphantly Penny joined the more advanced group of riders who were listening to a lecture on shoeing given by Mr Cartwright, the blacksmith. Then she went, with those members of Ride B who were not in the Branch jumping-team, for a mounted lesson, practising figures of eight, and 'bending' in-and-out of a row of upright poles.

Penny enjoyed the rally—everyone seemed so pleased with her.

'Now I'll really be able to make some jumping progress with Rusty,' she told her mother when she got home. 'So long as I put my hands through his neck-strap—so that I don't accidentally jab his mouth—we ought to be able to tackle some proper jumps. Yippee!'

EIGHT

Penny's lone adventure

DURING the last few days of the holidays Jane and Bernard helped Penny to make a bush jump. Bernard drove into the ground a couple of posts, a foot apart, and then put two more posts six feet away from them. To these four uprights he lashed a framework of bean-poles. The uprights and the bean-poles formed a container into which they stuffed gorse cut from the clump at the far end of the field. When they had finished they had a good brush-fence about two feet six inches high.

'Now we need some "wings",' said Jane. 'I know it's better, as a rule, not to use them so that one learns to place one's pony at the jump correctly without them, but Rusty may meet them sometime and so we ought to get him used to them. I know! We'll take the end two hurdles from the jumping lane.'

They made a second fence by hammering two more posts into the ground, and fixing a pole across them at a height of two feet nine. Bernard nailed a second pole underneath the first to make the jump look more solid.

'Now, Penny,' he said, 'try Rusty over those, and let's see how you get on.'

Rusty and Freckles had been watching the making of the jumps with interest, and when Rusty saw Penny bringing his bridle and saddle he came up to her at once, knowing that he would be sure of a fuss and perhaps a titbit or two if he did what was expected of him.

Penny mounted Rusty, let him sniff the jumps, and then rode him at the brush-fence. He still had a tendency to rush his jumps, and Penny hesitated to check him, because she did not want to put too much pressure on his reins and interfere with his mouth. Nevertheless, Rusty jumped the fence well. He took off in good time and, taking no chances with the prickly gorse, picked his feet well up and cleared it in great style.

He cantered on to the post-and-rails, but this time he seemed undecided where to take off and, jumping too late, blundered into the bar with his forelegs.

'Bad luck, Penny,' said Jane, picking up the bar and replacing it.

'Have another go,' urged Bernard.

Penny again rode Rusty at the jumps. He cleared the brushwood fence easily, but again misjudged his take-off, and brought down the top bar of the post-and-rails.

'I can't understand it,' said Bernard. 'I wouldn't have thought that the post-and-rails was any harder to jump than the brush. In fact, the brush is higher because the gorse comes at least six inches above the top bar. It must be quite three feet.'

'I know,' said Penny, reining up. 'But if you remember,

Bernard, it was a post-and-rails just like this one that Rusty had so much trouble in clearing in your field.'

'Oh, yes, the day I rapped him with the stick and he bolted.' Bernard looked chastened by the thought. 'I certainly do remember.'

'I think I know the reason,' said Jane. 'The brush fence is solid—three feet by six of packed gorse. It gives Rusty plenty to focus on. But a post-and-rails is a much more difficult jump for a pony to judge—particularly as it hasn't got any wings. How would it be if we put a low rail about six inches from the ground just in front of the jump? Then Rusty would be able to judge his distance more easily.'

They put a pole on the ground in front of the jump and, at once, it seemed that Jane had been right. Rusty cleared the post-and-rails without difficulty. Then Bernard and Jane mounted Corker and Freckles, and they all had a jolly time, competing against each other in jumping the fences.

The next day, however, Bernard and Jane had another Pony Club jumping practice, and Penny was left to ride

Rusty by herself. After jumping the obstacles three or four times, Penny rode up to the cottage. She wanted her mother to come out to see Rusty's progress.

'I'm sorry, dear.' Mrs Brooke was putting on her hat and coat. 'I can't come and watch Rusty now. Mrs Austin has just rung up. She wants me to go and help her to get the stalls ready for Cake-and-Apron Sale at the church hall this afternoon. I'm afraid you'll have to get your own lunch, but we'll all have a hot dinner tonight.'

Crest-fallen, Penny rode Rusty back to the field and watched as her mother hurried down the lane. She put Rusty over the jumps again, and then practised trotting a figure-of-eight. Rusty was dropping his head; he had lost his keenness, and twice he muffed the change of direction.

Penny sighed. 'I suppose you've had enough, Rusty,' she said, reining up and jumping down to put her head against her pony's. 'I don't blame you.' She stroked his nose. 'It's not much fun riding round the field on our own. I tell you what. You'd like a proper outing, and so would I.' She fastened him to the fence. 'Now you wait there. I'm going to cut up some sandwiches.'

Twenty minutes later, one pocket of her jacket bulging with a pack of cheese-and-tomato sandwiches, and the other stretched almost to bursting with two big chocolate wafers for herself and an apple for Rusty, Penny rode up the lane.

She cantered across the common and took the sandy path that curved past Huntsman's Hollow and Cherry Tree Farm. The sun was shining and the April breeze was speeding the fluffy clouds across the sky. Baby lambs were skipping in the field and the cherry orchard was white with blossom, while round the foot of the trees some late daffodils and white pheasant-eye narcissi made a pool on the grass, seeming to reflect the blossom above.

Penny rode on through the little village of Goosegreen where a dog ran from one of the cottages and barked at Rusty's heels, making him prance.

It was a wonderful ride and Penny was enjoying it. Rusty stepped out keenly, pleased to be seeing new ground. The sun was due south over the tower of Little Baybury church as they rode past, and, twenty minutes later, Penny halted Rusty by the wooden foot-bridge that led over Gayford Brook. Looping his reins over her arm, she sat on the stone wall in the sunshine, and began to share her lunch with him.

On the other side of the stream, the silver birches were just coming into leaf and, round their boles and by the mossy bank of the stream, primroses were in flower. After she and Rusty had finished eating, Penny picked a bunch of primroses to take home for her mother. She surrounded the posy with primrose leaves and tied it securely with a reed from the brook before putting it into her pocket.

'The primroses may get a bit squashed,' she told Rusty, 'but they'll soon freshen up in water and Mummy will love them, I know.'

She mounted again and they trotted on until they came to a fork where a signpost, pointing down the side-road, read *Millbrook ½ mile.*

'That's where Gay Fella lives,' Penny told Rusty, tickling his mane with her switch. 'I wonder how he is, and whether his leg's better. I'd love to see him and I don't think Ann Taylor would mind if we called . . . Come on, Rusty.'

Penny urged her pony to a trot and soon they came in sight of The Old Mill Stables where David Leslie kept his show jumpers. The mill house was white-washed and low, with a mossy grey roof. A row of stable-buildings faced it across a courtyard in which farm-carts had unloaded the grain. Behind the mill house was the leat, along the em-

bankment of which wood anemones, primroses and violets
nestled amid ivy leaves.

From the row of stable buildings, keen horsy heads looked
out. One of the horses, a big blue roan, neighed to Rusty who
answered. Penny looked along the loose-boxes. There was
the blue roan, a chestnut, and a grey, but where was Gay
Fella?

Penny rode into the courtyard and was just dismounting
to knock at the door of the mill house when there was a
crunch of hooves, and Gay Fella came round the corner led
by Ann Taylor.

'Oh, hello.' Ann's face broke into a smile. She seemed
pleased to see Penny. 'Where's your sister?'

'Jane's gone to a jumping practice with the Pony Club
team,' Penny explained, 'and Rusty and I were out for a
ride. I saw the signpost to Millbrook, so I thought I'd call
and see if Gay Fella was better. I hope you don't mind.' She
looked at Gay Fella. 'How is he?'

Ann Taylor straightened Gay Fella's mane, and gave his
glossy neck a fond pat. 'He's doing fine. As you can see, the

65

wound's healed, and now the vet says he is to have gentle walking exercise leading up to road-work. He'll be fit for the start of the summer season.'

'I should hope so,' said a young man's voice, and Penny found herself looking up at the face of David Leslie who had come, unnoticed, out of the house. He put a hand on Penny's shoulder. 'So you're one of the two young ladies whom I have to thank for rescuing Gay Fella.'

'Yes, I'm Penny Brooke,' Penny told him, and to cover her moment of shyness, pulled Rusty forward. 'And this is my pony, Rusty.'

'He's a likely-looking youngster.' David Leslie's knowledgeable gaze ran over Rusty, appraising the small, neat ears, kindly eye, pretty head, short neck, strong compact back and sturdy legs. 'Plenty of bone and spring there,' he said. 'What is he? Welsh?'

'That's right,' Penny nodded. 'He's only just four years old.'

'And just under fourteen hands.' David Leslie was still sizing up Rusty. 'Just right for the under fourteen-two classes, eh? He looks as if he could jump, too. Have you tried him?'

'Yes.' Penny related how she and Jane had been schooling Rusty over cavalletti; how she had gone in for the Pony Club test; failed, and then, after a lot of practice without stirrups and reins, passed, and how they had now made two proper jumps.

'Well then,' David Leslie smiled, 'I've got a paddock full of jumps just behind the stables. How about you putting Rusty over some of them and letting me see how he shapes?'

NINE

A chance of a lifetime

PENNY felt nervous as she rode Rusty into David Leslie's paddock. To jump in front of such a famous show jumper was an ordeal.

I'm sure to make a fool of myself, Penny thought. Perhaps I oughtn't to have come after all. Those jumps do look big.

She gave a sigh of relief as David Leslie and Ann went round lowering them to two feet nine.

'How's that?' David Leslie called after they had taken two rows of 'bricks' from the wall. 'Not too high now, are they?'

'I don't think so,' said Penny and, pulling herself together, rode Rusty round the course, showing him the jumps. Rusty looked at them calmly, but when Penny put him at the first jump, he fretted his bit until she, not wanting to interfere with his mouth, gave him his head. He dashed at the jump. It was a simple brush-fence and, in spite of coming at it too fast, and uncollected, Rusty gave a great heave of his hocks and got himself over without knocking down the bar.

The next jump was not so simple. It was a pair of parallel rails, but it had a row of bricks on the take-off side, enabling Rusty to judge his distance. Still jumping fast, he leapt 'big' and cleared it well. After that there was a post-and-rails, and a low triple with a wide spread. Rusty's speed helped him here and gave him the impetus needed to clear the triple bar.

Next came an in-and-out, and now Rusty's speed was his undoing. His leap carried him too far over the first part of the jump and so he got too near to the second part. Trying to check himself, he skidded on the soft ground and blundered into the rail, knocking it down, and throwing Penny on to his neck.

'Hard luck!' David Leslie ran to hold Rusty's head while Penny regained her seat. 'Not bad at all, though,' he went on, patting Rusty's neck. 'This pony can jump, sure enough.'

'I know,' Penny said and then added frankly, 'but I'm not very good. He'd do better with another rider.'

'Don't be discouraged,' said David Leslie. 'You've got a good seat for your age, but you're inclined to let Rusty rush his fences. I suggest you try to hold him back a bit.'

'I'm scared of jabbing his mouth,' said Penny. 'You see I used to "strap-hang" and I'm trying not to get back into the same bad habit.'

'I see what you mean.' David Leslie had listened with sympathetic attention, and now he was thinking about her problem. 'You won't be likely to jab Rusty's mouth so long as you keep your hands through his neck-strap,' he told her, 'but I think you'll have to use your reins to check his speed. You see, he simply races at his jumps.'

'I know,' Penny said. 'I expect it's because we used to get him to jump by putting titbits in his feed-box on the other side of the obstacle. He was so keen to get them that he rushed his jumps, and that's why he still does it.'

'Well, we can help you to overcome that.' David Leslie smiled across at his girl-groom. 'Can't we, Ann?'

'I should think so indeed,' Ann said cheerfully. 'We've just been having the same trouble with Sir Galahad, the colt which Mr Leslie bought from Ireland last Christmas. He rushes his fences.'

'So, if you'll come into the next field with us, Penny,' said David Leslie, 'we'll try to help you to cure Rusty.'

'Oh, thanks,' Penny said gratefully, 'but are you sure I'm not being a nuisance?'

'Indeed not,' David Leslie assured her. 'It's up to us horse-lovers to help each other. That's the rule of the stable.' He took them into another paddock where a row of three cavalletti led to a two feet six jump.

'What a good idea!' said Penny. 'Jane and I never thought of finishing off the row of cavalletti with a bigger jump. I suppose that having to jump the cavalletti first slows the pony down before he takes the jump.'

'That's it,' David Leslie nodded. 'He has to jump the cavalletti slowly and carefully, and so he approaches the bigger jumps in the same way. After a while,' he went on, 'you can vary the sequence and have only one or two cavalletti before the bigger jump, but put another cavalletti and another jump on the far side. If you change your obstacles round from time to time, your pony will learn to jump slowly and warily—to think and look before he leaps, in fact. You'll find it a big help when you come on to show jumping.'

Show jumping! Penny thought. There was not much hope of that. Even if her father would let her, she did not think she would ever be good enough. All the same, the rest of the afternoon passed very happily.

After a further three quarters of an hour's schooling for Rusty, David Leslie had to leave them. He had arranged to drive to Easthampton to sign some copies of his latest show jumping book. But Ann was not going anywhere, so she showed Penny round the stables, and introduced her to all the horses.

While Rusty, his girth slackened and a borrowed rug over his back, had a small feed of pony-cubes, bran and chopped carrots to get him ready for the ride home, Penny went indoors with Ann for a glass of milk and two chunky slices of fruit cake.

The clock on the tower of Little Baybury church was just striking five when Penny and Rusty rode past half an hour later.

'Goodness!' Penny said to her pony. 'The afternoon has gone quickly, and we've got an eight-mile ride before we're home.' She urged her pony to a trot. 'Come on, Rusty.'

When Penny reached home it was a quarter past six and her father, her mother—back from the Cake and Apron Sale—and Jane, were just sitting down to their steak and chips.

'Where've you been, Penny?' Mrs Brooke asked. 'I've been quite worried. I guessed you'd gone for a ride because Rusty wasn't in the field.'

Before Penny had a chance to speak Jane put in her admonition: 'You really are the end, Penny! I do think you ought to have left a note to say where you'd gone.'

'Yes, suppose you'd had an accident,' added Mr Brooke. 'None of us would have known where to start looking for you. In future you're not to go for long rides on your own without letting your mother or I know where you're going.'

'Fair enough, Daddy,' Penny said. 'I'm sorry. But please, don't be cross with me because that would spoil everything.'

'And your steak and chips will be spoiled, too,' Mrs Brooke told her. 'Your plate's in the bottom oven. You'd better go and get it before it's all dried up.'

'Very well, Mummy.'

Penny's spirits were too high for her to be subdued by her family's disapproval and, as she sat down at the table, she told them what an exciting afternoon she'd had.

'You'd never guess where I've been.' She paused. 'I've seen Gay Fella! I've been to the Old Mill Stables.'

'David Leslie's place!' Jane stopped eating. 'Well, of all things! Fancy sneaking off there when I hadn't got a chance to go with you.'

'Oh Jane, it wasn't like that,' Penny said. 'It would have been even more fun if you had been able to come. Then you and Freckles could have had a jumping lesson, too.'

Jane gaped. 'You don't mean to say that David Leslie's been teaching you to jump? How did you get on? I hope you didn't disgrace us.'

'I thought I was doing at first,' Penny confessed, 'but somehow Mr Leslie seemed to think I was quite good. He said that Rusty tended to rush his fences, but he took him in hand to cure that. He gave me a lot of useful tips, and—best of all—' she went on, her voice rising with excitement— 'Mr Leslie confirmed what we've always thought . . . He said Rusty had the making of a first-class show jumping pony.'

Mr Brooke almost choked on his last chip. Resisting Jane's well-meant attempt to pat him between the shoulders, he took a gulp of coffee, cleared his throat and looked sternly at Penny.

'I thought I'd told you to put all that show jumping nonsense out of your head,' he said. 'I've warned you that it's too expensive. It'd mean buying all sorts of kit, and hiring horse-boxes to take you and Rusty over half the country, and then there would be the entrance fees.'

'There might be prize-money, too, Daddy,' Penny pointed out.

'Some hopes!' exclaimed Mr Brooke. 'What chance do you think you and Rusty would have against all these blue-blooded ponies and semi-professional child-riders who have been at the game since they were six or seven years old? Besides that, it's dangerous—or so your mother says. She'd never give me a moment's peace if she thought I was going to let you go in for show jumping.'

Penny looked pleadingly at her mother. 'But, Mummy—'

'It's no use, dear.' Mrs Brooke was firm. 'I *should* worry. It's silly, I know, but I shouldn't be able to help it.'

'Anyway it isn't going to arise,' Mr Brooke said, closing the discussion. 'We're going to have no show jumping in this family.'

TEN

Jim lends a hand

'WE'D never be good enough for show jumping anyway,' Jane said to Penny later that evening as they were saying good night to the ponies.

'I suppose you're right,' sighed Penny. She patted Rusty. 'You might have made a show jumper though. It's a shame that you can't have your chance.' She turned to Jane. 'Well, we can still jump in the field, and you and Freckles will be jumping in the Pony Club competitions.'

'Yes,' said Jane, 'and I'm going to need some more obstacles. Freckles will have to jump a full course in the competitions, so she ought to be practising regularly. Once a week, on Saturdays, isn't enough.'

Next day, after church, Jane and Penny worked on their jumping course. In addition to the brush-fence and the post-and-rails that they had already made, they built a pair of parallel bars, standing the poles on oil-drums and putting a row of stones on the ground just in front of the jump to

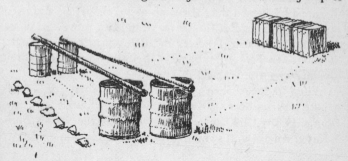

make a base-line. Then they placed three large wooden boxes on end to form a 'wall'.

'We'll pick out the jumps in black and white paint,' said Jane, 'and then the ponies will see them more easily.'

Penny nodded.

Jane looked thoughtfully at the obstacles. 'We've got four jumps so far,' she said. 'We'll need several more, of course, but for the moment we can add the cavalletti in a row down this side to make a "grid". The ponies will have to jump in and out of them and that will steady Rusty. When he knows that he's coming to a "trappy" obstacle like that, he won't be so inclined to rush.'

They placed the five cavalletti in a row, nine feet apart from each other so as to fit Freckles' and Rusty's strides. Jane and Penny rode Freckles and Rusty round the course first in a right-handed circuit and then in a left.

'Not bad,' conceded Bernard next Sunday afternoon when he saw the course for the first time, 'but you could do with some more obstacles.' He thought for a moment, then said: 'I know, how about a tree-trunk? There's a beauty in Wyatt's field. Just big enough to make the ponies spread themselves well.'

Jane asked the farmer whether they might have the fallen trunk and he said that they could, so she and Penny and Bernard harnessed their three ponies to the trunk and tried to drag it home. But the trunk would not move. Strain as they might, Corker, Freckles and Rusty just could not make it budge. So Penny ran back to the farm to ask the help of the farmer's son, young Jim Wyatt.

When he heard their predicament, Jim grinned. 'This is where an iron horse can do better than a four-legged one, young Penny,' he said, moving towards the farm's blue-painted tractor and swinging its engine. 'Up you get.'

With Penny and Jim aboard, the tractor chugged over the fields until they came to the place where the three ponies, encouraged by Bernard and Jane, were still struggling to move the tree-trunk.

'Unhitch your steeds,' Jim called above the noise of the tractor's engine. 'Stand clear.'

He jumped down from the tractor and expertly fixed a chain round the trunk of the fallen tree. Climbing back on to the tractor-seat, he let in the clutch and the tractor moved forward, its deeply-treaded tyres biting into the ground and enabling it to haul forward the big tree-trunk.

Soon the trunk was in position as an obstacle, making up Jane's and Penny's home-made jumping course.

'Six fences, eh?' Jim said, his freckled face breaking into a smile as he sized up the jumps. 'You three have done well. If you had another couple of jumps it really would be a full course. I tell you what—we've got a pair of sheep hurdles lying idle down at the farm. If you like, you can borrow them until next lambing season.' He got back aboard the tractor. 'I'll fetch them for you now.'

He brought back two bales of straw as well as the hurdles and placed them on top of each other to make an extra jump.

'That's a super idea, Jim,' Penny approved delightedly. 'Now we've got nine jumps.'

'That's right,' Jim nodded. 'But we want to think carefully before we decide where to put these hurdles. According to all the show jumping I've seen on the telly, it's important to have a change of direction in a jumping-course.'

'So it is,' Bernard agreed. He thought for a moment. 'Well, how would it be if we started at the end of the field with the brush-fence, cut across diagonally to jump the tree-trunk, put one of the hurdles slantwise just round the corner so that we had to swing round quite sharply to take it? Then we could go diagonally over the parallel bars and the post-and-rails, turn again and take the wall and the bales of straw, and come straight down the far side over the cavalletti and the other hurdle.'

'So that the course would be like a figure-of-eight,' Jane nodded. 'I get the idea.'

'Wonderful!' exclaimed Penny. 'And maybe we might even find some more oil-drums and larch poles and build a triple just to finish off with.'

'No sooner said than done,' smiled Jim, 'or nearly done,

anyway. There are quite a lot of empty oil-drums at the farm and I dare say I could find three more poles.' He started the tractor again. 'I'll go and see what I can do.'

During the next week Jane and Penny jumped Rusty and Freckles twice round the course before going in to do their homework. They jumped on Saturday morning too and in the afternoon when Jane had ridden off with Bernard to go to the Pony Club team's jumping practice, Penny raised some of the jumps to just over three feet.

'There, Rusty,' she told her pony, patting him before climbing back into the saddle. 'That'll put you on your mettle. Now we'll see what you really can do.'

The jumps were now quite big for a pony, but Rusty was nearly fourteen hands and he was a powerful jumper with plenty of natural spring and strength in his short back and sturdy hocks, and after a warming-up canter he tackled the jumps collectedly as they came—first the brush-fence and tree-trunk; then a sharp turn to take the upright hurdle. Next the parallel bars and the post-and-rails. Penny swung him round to jump the 'wall' and the bales of straw. Then came the 'grid' of cavalletti at eighteen inches from the ground.

Rusty checked his speed and jumped carefully in-and-out down the line of four. Then, with an increase of speed, he cleared the last hurdle.

'Well done!' called a voice from the road, as Penny pulled up and turned in surprise to see David Leslie and Ann Taylor watching from the gate. She waved and rode Rusty up to them. In the lane David Leslie's black sports car was parked, and Ann had a gay scarf over her fair hair to protect her 'set' from the wind.

'We were just driving into Easthampton to pick up a new saddle,' Ann told Penny. 'We saw you jumping as we came along the main road, so we turned up the lane to see how Rusty was getting on.'

'And I must say,' David Leslie put in, 'that he seems to be doing splendidly. The great thing now, Penny, will be to see that you don't over-face him or let him get bored. You should expect him to take biggish jumps like these only occasionally. For routine schooling, two feet six is enough for a pony his size.'

Penny nodded. 'I only put the jumps higher for this afternoon. I wanted to see what Rusty really could do—'

'And you must be very pleased with the result,' Ann said with an encouraging smile. 'David's right though—if Rusty jumps every day without a break he'll get stale.'

'I know,' Penny agreed. 'It's difficult in the week now we're back at school. In the evening we have to do our homework and so there's time only for half an hour or so of riding. But, at the weekends, we do try to get in a ride round the lanes as well.'

'That's the idea,' David Leslie said, 'and if you could manage it without upsetting any farmers, try Rusty over one or two natural obstacles—ditches, little hedges, posts-and-rails. Cross-country jumping of that sort will make him handy and ready to face anything. Then get in as much road work as you can manage with plenty of walking to build up his muscles. Riding sometimes at a sitting-trot, without rising, will leave more weight on his loins and will also help. You should soon have him ready to try one or two shows.'

'The Broomwood Red Cross Fête has children's jumping

classes,' Ann told Penny. 'Why not try him there?'

'I can't,' Penny explained with a heavy sigh. 'Daddy won't hear of Jane and me doing any show jumping.'

'But the Broomwood Fête isn't what you'd really call a *show*,' Ann pointed out. 'It's just one or two riding and jumping classes for the under-fourteens—something to draw in the people who enjoy watching children and their ponies.'

'Why doesn't your father want you to show jump, Penny?' David Leslie asked, his grey eyes studying Penny's face shrewdly. 'I suppose he must have a good reason.'

'Oh, he has,' Penny assured them, downcast. 'The best of reasons. He says he simply can't afford it. You see Daddy's not rich. In fact we're quite hard up, and Daddy has to work all hours, going out to repair people's television sets and radios.'

'So your father must be Mr Brooke of G. Brooke, Radio and Television.' David Leslie smiled across at Ann. 'I must call at his shop sometime. Our aerial needs re-zoning—it swung round in that gale we had last week.'

'I'm sure Daddy will be pleased to help you,' Penny told him. 'And I know he'll do it well. He's a very clever television engineer.'

'I'm sure he is.' David Leslie got back into the car, and gave Penny a friendly smile. 'We'll be off now, but I expect we'll be seeing you again. Meanwhile keep up the good work with Rusty.'

ELEVEN

Daddy springs a surprise

THAT Saturday, Mr and Mrs Brooke were late getting home from the shop, so Jane was back from the Pony Club practice before them. After she and Penny had turned Freckles into the field with Rusty and watched her enjoy a roll, the two girls went into the cottage to get ready for tea.

By a quarter past six Mr and Mrs Brooke had not returned, and Jane and Penny began to set the table.

'Let's make Mummy and Daddy something tasty as a surprise,' Penny suggested.

Jane opened the pantry door, and looked round the shelves. 'What is there? . . . Hm! . . . some cold potatoes and cheese and two slices of cold ham. I know!' She collected the ingredients capably and carried them to the kitchen table. 'Get me a mixing bowl, Penny.'

'What are you going to make?' Penny asked, interested.

'I'll chop up this ham and mix it into the potatoes with some milk,' Jane explained. 'Then I'll shape it into rounds, roll them in bread-crumbs and fry them.'

'What about the cheese?' Penny prompted.

'We'll have a cheese-sauce,' Jane told her. 'It's quite easy to make with milk and cornflour and grated cheese, and I'll open that packet of frozen beans that Mummy's got in the fridge.'

'Ham-and-potato cakes, runner beans and cheese sauce,' Penny said. 'They'll love it.'

Everything seemed to go right. The ham-and-potato cakes fried to a golden brown without burning or sticking to the pan. The cornflour mixed smoothly and, when Jane stirred it into the milk and added the grated cheese, it thickened without lumps. Penny had just tasted a slice of runner bean and said that it was tender when they heard Mr Brooke's van turn into the drive.

'You're just in time,' Penny said as her mother and father walked in. 'We've cooked you a surprise, and it's ready to put on the table.'

'It smells tasty,' said Mr Brooke, smiling at his daughter.

'And I'm longing for a cup of tea,' said Mrs Brooke. 'I'm ready to drop.'

'Well, all you've got to do is to drop into a chair, Mummy,' said Jane, pouring out some tea. 'Here, this'll pull you round.'

Soon everybody was eating the meal that Jane had cooked.

'I don't know when I've enjoyed my tea so much,' said Mrs Brooke, putting down her knife and fork at last. 'It was beautifully cooked.'

'Yes, thank you both very much.' Mr Brooke stood up and began to stack the plates.

Jane took them from him. 'We'll clear away, and wash up,' she said firmly. 'All you and Mummy have to do is to move over to your arm-chairs and take it easy.'

Feeling pleased that their surprise had been such a success, the two girls very willingly carried the dishes into the kitchen.

As they did so they heard their father say jokingly to their mother: 'Well, dear, this seems to be where we sit back a bit and get the benefit of having daughters. Now that they're older they seem as though they're going to be a boon about the house.'

'Yes, it's wonderful,' agreed Mrs Brooke. 'But I must say I feel guilty sitting here and letting them do all the washing up after they got the tea ready as well.'

'Oh, relax, Mummy,' Jane said, coming in to fold up the table-cloth. 'It'll spoil everything if you're going to sit on the edge of your chair feeling you ought to be up and doing. For goodness' sake, sit back and enjoy yourself.'

'That's an order,' Mr Brooke said, with a wink. He pushed the stool across to his wife. 'Here you are, dear. Put up your feet.'

When Penny came back into the sitting-room, her mother was comfortably reading a magazine while her father was looking into the fire.

'I've been thinking about what we were discussing at the shop this afternoon,' Mr Brooke said, looking across at his wife.

'So have I.' Mrs Brooke put down her magazine. 'I haven't really been reading a word.'

Jane had now come into the room and Penny looked across at her, baffled. What were Mummy and Daddy talking about?

'Do you think we ought to tell them?' Mr Brooke asked.

Mrs Brooke was silent for a time before she answered: 'Yes, I do. You begin, George.'

'Tell us what?' Penny asked, mystified. 'We're in suspense.'

'Well, the fact is,' said Mr Brooke, 'we had quite a long chat with David Leslie this afternoon. He came into the shop.'

'Oh yes,' said Penny. 'He said he would.'

'I was certainly glad to see him,' said Mr Brooke, 'because I've been wanting for a long time to have a talk with someone who really knows about this pony jumping business.'

'And what did he say?' Penny asked.

'Well, we told him how we felt about not letting you take the ponies to shows because of the expense,' said Mr Brooke.

'And he was very understanding,' Mrs Brooke added. 'He said he knew exactly how we felt, but that lots of children went in for little local shows and gymkhanas without it costing very much.'

'About half a crown entrance fee to each class,' Jane said.

'That's right.' Mr Brooke looked from one to the other of his daughters. 'So you see, it's really a matter of you two making your pocket-money stretch that far.'

'Do you really mean you'll let us go in for local shows, Daddy?' Penny gazed at her father unable to believe her ears.

'Well, yes—if you're careful.'

Penny bounced to her father's chair, and sitting on the arm put her cheek against his. 'Oh, you are a wonderful Daddy!'

Jane and Penny practised jumping harder than ever. Bernard often jumped with them and soon the field became muddy and churned-up.

'I don't think we can expect Freckles and Rusty to go on grazing here now that it's a jumping paddock,' Jane said one evening after they had unsaddled the ponies. 'It's such a small field and now there's more mud than grass.'

'What are we going to do then?' Penny asked.

'Find another field, of course,' Jane told her. 'I'll ask Mr Wyatt in the morning if we can use one of his.'

'We'd have to pay something for the grazing,' Penny pointed out.

'I know,' Jane said. 'But what else can we do? If we don't find new grazing Rusty and Freckles will have to be given extra feeds. And that would cost even more, besides being not nearly as good for them as fresh grass. A change of grazing is a very good thing for a pony. All fields get tired and pony-sick in time.'

Next day was a Friday, and, in the evening, instead of riding the ponies as usual, Jane and Penny went down to the farm to see Mr Wyatt.

The farmer looked thoughtful when he heard what the girls had to say. 'Aye,' he said at last, rubbing his head. 'I doubt if it would do much harm if you put your ponies in Three-Acre with our old Captain. Mind you, you'll have to watch 'em for a while to make sure they don't get awkward with each other. Horses and ponies can be cussed creatures when they're new to each other. So it's best to keep an eye on 'em until they get properly acquainted. We don't want them kicking and biting each other, do we? That wouldn't help you to win any prizes at the Broomwood Fête.'

'We'll be on our guard against that, Mr Wyatt,' Jane assured him. 'Now, how much shall we pay you for the field?'

Mr Wyatt shook his head. 'I reckon pony-riding's an expensive enough business for two young girls like you, as it is. I don't want to take your money for the field, but I'll tell you what—it would help our Granny if you would give her a hand with her poultry every Saturday morning, cleaning out the pens and such.'

'Fair enough,' Jane agreed readily.

Next morning Jane and Penny put on their old jeans and shirts and hurried down to the Wyatts' farm to report for duty. It was hard and dirty work—worse than mucking out a stable, but the girls did it willingly.

After they had brushed down the boards and roosting perches and cleared out all the old litter from the floor, they spread out fresh peat-moss litter and put sweet-smelling hay in the nest boxes. Then they changed the water in the drinking troughs and, followed by a flock of happily-clucking, free-range hens, they scattered corn over the grass to encourage them to scratch.

That afternoon there was no jumping practice for the Pony Club team. So Jane, Bernard and Penny went for a long picnic-ride. When they got back, the girls unsaddled Rusty and Freckles and turned them into Mr Wyatt's Three-Acre field at the far end of which Captain was already grazing — near a pond. The ponies walked into the middle of the field and then rolled, easing their backs where their saddles had been. Then they got up and began to graze while Jane and Penny walked round the boundary, making sure that there were no gaps in the hedge.

Captain took no notice of the new-comers, but, when Jane and Penny came back to the field a little while later after taking their bridles and saddles to the farm, they saw that he was standing, nose-to-tail with Freckles on one side and Rusty on the other, their tails swishing to keep away each other's midges.

'Look,' said Penny. 'They've made friends.'

During the next fortnight Jane and Penny worked hard to get Freckles and Rusty into tiptop condition. Every evening, after they had done their homework, they took the ponies for an hour's road-exercise, riding them mainly at a walk and sitting-trot to improve their muscles, but fitting in a sharp canter or two on the common, and ending with two or three jumps in the field behind Orchard Cottage.

On the Saturday before the fête, Jane, as usual, went to the Pony Club practice, and Penny decided to act on David Leslie's advice and take Rusty for a cross-country ride. She knew that Mr Wyatt would not mind her riding across his fields to Bunbury Heath. From there she could circle back through Updean Woods, which had always been open to riders, and then come home slowly through the village, giving Rusty a chance to cool off.

Rusty was keen and put in a couple of bucks as he cantered across the first field, but he took the low hedge at the end of the Home Meadow without fault, and galloped on down the Seven-Acre, only pulling with impatience when Penny got down to remove the top rail of a high post-and-rails, leaving the lower one for him to jump.

Rusty backed and pulled when Penny got off to replace the rail and would not stand still for her to mount. However, by shortening his left rein so that he could move only in a circle, she managed to hold him long enough to get into the saddle. Almost before she had found her off-stirrup, Rusty was away and galloping down the grassy ride along Huntsman's Spinney with Penny having to duck her head level with his shoulder to avoid the overhanging branches.

At the end of the spinney was a narrow brook in front of a quickthorn hedge—a difficult jump for an inexperienced pony. Coming at it fast, Rusty flew both brook and hedge and pecked only slightly on landing. They were in the open country now and Penny pulled up Rusty for a breather before letting him canter up the long slope to the ridge of Bunbury Heath.

Taking their time, Rusty and Penny trotted and cantered over the heath-land, jumping a drainage ditch and a fallen tree on the way.

Soon they came to the entrance of Updean Woods. Beside the white gate was a notice saying: *Horsemen are welcome to ride in these woods provided they keep to the paths.*

The gate was too big for Rusty to jump so Penny had to dismount to open it. They trotted along the main ride between the smooth-boled beech trees, with ferns on either side and drifts of bluebells making a smoky mist over the ground.

In the wood there were several chances to jump. There was a brook, the trunks of two felled trees and, leading into another ride, a not-too-high post-and-rails which Rusty jumped easily.

'Well done,' Penny said to Rusty, rewarding him with a pat.

She was pleased with him. He was jumping well and seemed to be in fine condition and not too blown or tired by the cross-country ride.

Penny was in a confident mood when they came to the end of the woods and saw an easy stile beside the gate leading out of the estate.

'I'm sure we could jump that stile, Rusty.' Penny took a 'feel' on her reins and leaned forward to set him at the jump.

Rusty took off just right, and Penny felt a thrill as he cleared the stile. Then, just as he was landing, a sheep skittered up from the ditch on the other side and collided with Rusty. Rusty somersaulted, while the sheep ran away, unhurt, and Penny was thrown through the air to land several yards away.

Without even wondering whether she was hurt, Penny

scrambled to her feet and ran to where Rusty, on his back with his legs in the air, was rolling and kicking trying to get to his feet.

Penny grasped his trailing reins and stood clear while Rusty, with a final roll, heaved himself over and got up. His saddle, the broken girth trailing, slipped to the ground.

'Are you hurt, Rusty?' Penny anxiously examined her pony and felt up and down his legs. She could not feel any injury and he did not wince.

Penny patted Rusty to reassure him and went to pick up her saddle. It looked twisted and lumpy. She lifted it. The saddle bent in the middle, and, dismayed, she turned it over to see a point of wood sticking through the serge lining. The saddle-tree was broken.

'Oh, Rusty!' Penny, near to tears, turned to her pony. 'This was only an old saddle to begin with; we had it re-stuffed and made the best of it, but it's done for now, and new saddles cost the earth—a hundred pounds at least. I'll never be able to have a new one. There'll be no jumping for you at the Broomwood Fête now!'

TWELVE

Treasure trove

'WELL, that's the last straw,' said Mr Brooke as Penny told him the sad story of the broken saddle. 'I can't afford to buy you another one.'

'I know.' Penny sighed. 'Everything's hopeless. There'll be no chance now of riding Rusty in the Broomwood Fête.'

'Surely *something* could be done with the saddle,' Mrs Brooke suggested. 'Couldn't it be mended?'

'It wouldn't be worth it, Mummy,' said Jane. 'It's such an old, patched-up saddle. It'd cost a lot to have it mended, and even then it might be a bad fit.'

'Then I don't know what we can do.' Mrs Brooke looked worried. 'We haven't been able to afford any extras for a long time now. You see, people haven't been buying many television sets lately.'

'And the disc-trade hasn't been as good as we'd hoped when we fitted up the listening booths,' Mr Brooke added. 'Teenagers come and listen and lark about, but they don't buy much. I'm sorry, chick. But I'm having quite a struggle, as it is.'

Penny looked round the room. 'Isn't there anything we don't want that we could sell?'

'Oh yes!' Mrs Brooke said cynically. 'My ermine, my pearls and my diamond tiara!' She broke off, and looked thoughtful. 'Wait a minute—perhaps Penny's suggestion isn't so silly after all.' She looked across at Mr Brooke. 'What about Granny's treasures?'

Mr Brooke sat up. 'That's an idea. I'd forgotten about the family heirlooms.'

'What heirlooms?' Jane asked, intrigued.

'What treasures?' Penny demanded excitedly.

Mr Brooke did not answer. He was busy thinking.

He turned to Mrs Brooke. 'I doubt if they would fetch the money we need to buy Penny a saddle, but we could try.'

'Of course we'd intended to keep them for the girls until they were twenty-one,' said Mrs Brooke, 'though I'm sure Granny wouldn't have minded them being sold to buy a saddle when Penny needs one so badly.'

'Granny's treasures!' Penny's face lit up. 'Oh, I think I know what they are. Where are they now?'

Mr Brooke produced his key-ring, and selected a small silvery key which he handed to Penny. 'They're in the left-hand top drawer of your mother's dressing-table.'

'Right at the back,' said Mrs Brooke, 'wrapped in a piece of black velvet.'

Penny ran upstairs, opened the drawer and came back with a small bundle. She put it on the table and they all stood round to see. Penny folded back the velvet, and there— glowing in the rays of the evening sun—were Granny's treasures—a fob watch, a string of pearls, an amethyst brooch and Granny's wedding ring.

Penny felt sad for a moment. 'I remember how Granny used to wear these.'

'So do I, dear,' said her mother, and was quiet for a while before she added: 'Now, Jane, what are we going to do? Half of these really belong to you. But we'd probably have to sell all of them to get enough money to buy a saddle for Penny.'

Jane gazed at the treasures. She had always admired the

pearls and the ring, and they had never looked so lovely as they did now.

She turned away and saw Granny's photograph on the mantelpiece. Then suddenly she heard herself saying: 'Sell them all,' and so that she wouldn't be tempted to change her mind she hurriedly folded the velvet over the jewellery and handed the bundle to her father.

On Monday, when Mr Brooke came home from the shop, Jane and Penny were waiting anxiously to hear whether he had been able to sell the treasures.

'Any luck, Daddy?' Jane called, running to the van as her father got out.

Mr Brooke nodded. 'I took them to the jeweller in Church Street,' he began.

'How much did he give you, Daddy?' Penny broke in eagerly.

'Not as much as we'd hoped, chick,' Mr Brooke said. 'As a matter of fact it was sixty pounds.' He noticed the crest-fallen look on Penny's face, and patted her shoulder. 'Cheer up, love. New saddles may cost more than that, but we might be able to get a good second-hand one for less. After tea we'll go to see Mr Shaw at the riding school, and ask him what he advises. He might even have a saddle for sale.'

Mr Shaw looked thoughtful when he heard the reason for the Brooke family's visit.

'Well, I usually have a saddle or two to spare,' he told them. 'But I don't know whether I'd be doing you a good turn if I were to sell you one of them. For a beginner, a perfectly-fitting saddle isn't perhaps so important, but young Penny here's becoming quite an advanced rider, so I hear, and the right saddle would make all the difference to her progress—and to Rusty's comfort, too. It's true that you can make any saddle fit by using sheepskin pads so long as it's roughly the right size for the pony, but sooner or later the saddle slips about and the pony gets a sore back.'

'What are we to do then?' Mrs Brooke wanted to know. 'How much would a new saddle cost?'

'You'd get a pony-saddle of sorts for about eighty pounds,' said Mr Shaw, 'complete with irons and leathers. But the cheapest isn't always the least expensive in the long run, y'know. A cheap saddle often has a poor lining which takes a long time to dry and sometimes goes lumpy. Apart from that, now that Penny's going in for jumping, she needs a really well-cut saddle—a forward-seat saddle, and they cost more. Then she'll need safety bars and raw-hide leathers. Cheap leathers sometimes break and can cause a nasty fall.'

Jane nodded in agreement. 'I've just had the buckles moved on Freckles' stirrup leathers,' she told Mr Shaw.

'Very wise,' approved the riding master, 'because if, as most people do, you always ride with the buckle in the same hole, there's a strain on the leather that might cause it to break. As soon as you find the stirrup iron has worn a crease-mark into the leather, you should go to the saddler and get him to move the buckle so that the wear comes on fresh leather.'

'That's interesting,' said Mr Brooke. 'But about Penny's saddle. We can't afford to pay more than eighty pounds at the outside.'

'So what on earth can we do, Mr Shaw?' asked Mrs Brooke.

'It seems as though I shan't have a saddle after all.' Penny could not hide her disappointment.

'Oh, it's not as bad as that, Penny.' Mr Shaw's tone was

encouraging. 'There are one or two firms which specialize in really good second-hand saddles. As a matter of fact I'm going to London on Wednesday to try to find a couple of bridles so, if you like, I'll see what I can find for you. I'll have a look at Rusty tomorrow to see how he's grown so that I can get some idea of the fit, and then I'll bring back a saddle for you to try. The firm is very obliging and, if the saddle should happen not to be right they'll change it for you—in fact, they'll go on changing it until you are suited.'

'That sounds fair enough,' said Mrs Brooke gratefully. 'I'm glad we came to you for advice.'

The saddle that Mr Shaw brought back from London for Penny cost fifty-five pounds and was well-cut and leather-lined. It would, as he explained, always keep its shape, be easy to clean with warm water and saddle soap, and would soon dry. It had safety catches for the raw-hide stirrup-leathers, and stainless steel irons which left plenty of room for Penny's feet to move freely.

Mr Shaw had chosen a nylon girth which did away with

the need for two girths and, being made of several separate nylon cords, was non-slip, easy to wash and, most important, would allow Rusty's skin to breathe freely and to perspire and so would not become caked with sweat and likely to cause a girth-gall. To try on the saddle, Mr Shaw first put a blanket over Rusty. Then he fitted the saddle and told Penny to ride several times round the field. After ten minutes he took off the saddle and the blanket showed the impression of the side-bars. Mr Shaw, Jane and Penny saw that they had pressed evenly from front to rear.

'So far—so good,' said Mr Shaw, removing the blanket, replacing the saddle and telling Penny to mount again. 'Now we must make sure that there is no pressure on Rusty's shoulder blades.' He passed his hand under the front of the saddle. 'Come on, Jane,' he added, 'I'd like you to lift Rusty's near-fore as high as you can.'

Jane did as she was told, and Mr Shaw looked pleased.

'Put his foot down again now,' he said and explained to Jane and Penny the reason for this. 'If there was too much

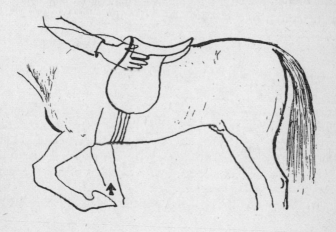

pressure on Rusty's shoulders my hand would have been pinched when Jane picked up Rusty's foot. As it is there's plenty of room on the shoulders and also on either side of the withers.' He ran his hand round the back of the saddle and found that there was room enough for the flat of his hand under the cantle. 'This saddle's a good fit,' he pronounced. 'It's not too tight and so it won't rub or pinch Rusty. On the other hand, it's not too big, and so it won't slip about, and give him a sore back.'

'It feels comfortable to me, too,' said Penny, dismounting and patting Rusty before turning to thank Mr Shaw. 'You must have been to a lot of trouble to find such a marvellous saddle for Rusty, Mr Shaw,' she said gratefully. 'It is kind of you.'

'And I'm looking forward to seeing you ride on it at the Broomwood Fête,' Mr Shaw told her, smiling. 'Some of my best pupils are going in for the under-fourteen class, so I'm warning you, young lady, you won't have it all your own way. It may be only a small local show, but there'll be some stiff competition. It'll put you and Rusty on your mettle!'

THIRTEEN

The sixth fence

RUSTY seemed to like his new saddle, and Penny quickly got used to it. She found that, with its deeper seat and forward-cut panels, it was more comfortable for jumping.

After Rusty's fright at the stile, Penny had wondered what would happen when she asked him to jump again. But, to her relief, he did not seem to have had his confidence shaken and he happily negotiated the home-made course.

Soon it was Friday—the eve of the fête.

'Homework can wait till Sunday,' Penny said after tea, in response to her mother's inquiry. 'Jane and I are going to do some tack-cleaning ready for tomorrow.'

'And we've got to clean out Granny Wyatt's hen-houses,' added Jane. 'We shan't have time to do them in the morning.'

When Jane and Penny had done their poultry chores, they inspected Rusty and Freckles in the Three-Acre field and took them a short feed of pony-nuts and chaff. Then they collected their saddles and bridles from the farm and carried them home to clean.

After breakfast, next morning they went to the farm to catch their ponies and bring them up to the cottage to groom them. As Penny was picking up Rusty's near-fore foot to clean it out with the hoof-pick, she noticed, to her dismay, a slight crack at the side of his hoof.

'Look, Jane!' She showed her sister.

'Goodness!' said Jane. 'You mustn't jump Rusty until that crack's been treated.'

'Oh dear!' Penny gasped, 'and the show is this afternoon. Whatever shall I do?'

'Take Rusty to the smithy. Hurry! You haven't much time.'

Quickly Penny saddled and bridled Rusty. Of all the bad luck, she thought as she set off, having to ride Rusty all the way to Rompton and back just when she wanted him to be fresh for the show.

It seemed a long way to the smithy because Penny, not wanting to lengthen the crack in Rusty's hoof, took him steadily—mostly at a walk. At last they got there, but they had to wait while Mr Cartwright finished shoeing another pony.

The smith examined Rusty's hoof.

'Well, I am surprised at this happening to a pony of yours, miss,' he said, looking up at Penny. 'It seems to me that you've forgotten to oil his hooves regularly. This hoof's quite brittle and that's why it's cracked.'

'Yes, that's right,' Penny admitted. 'I haven't oiled his hooves for weeks.'

'And now you've learned your lesson,' said Mr Cartwright. 'Pick out your pony's feet and oil his hooves every day. There's nothing like hoof-oil to preserve the hooves and keep a hoof healthy and growing. Now, never forget—the most important thing about a pony is his feet. No foot—no pony, as the saying is!'

'I am sorry, Mr Cartwright,' Penny said, ashamed. 'Will you be able to stop the crack? You see, I want to jump Rusty at the fête this afternoon.'

'I'll do my best,' said the blacksmith. 'But if you'd left it any longer, or if the crack had run across the hoof instead of

being vertical or if it had been deeper—well, then it'd have been a job for the vet.'

Penny watched as Mr Cartwright heated a small iron in the fire. She held Rusty's head while the smith burned a small V above the crack. Rusty's hoof smoked and he twitched, laying back his ears. He could not feel any pain because the hoof-wall is insensitive, but the smoke and the sizzle alarmed him.

'Steady, Rusty,' Penny soothed. 'It's all over now.' She turned to Mr Cartwright. 'Will I be able to jump him this afternoon?'

'You will,' said Mr Cartwright and smiled. 'And the best of luck to the pair of you.'

It seemed as though all the pony-owners in the district were taking their mounts to Broomwood Fête that afternoon. On the way, Jane, Penny and Bernard passed several groups of riders, and always there seemed to be the noise of hooves ahead, making Rusty quicken his pace and fret his bit, wanting to catch up with the ponies ahead.

By the time that they reached the showground, Rusty was damp with sweat and Penny was hot and flushed from trying to hold him back.

'I suppose it's only natural for Rusty to be excited,' Penny said, trying to make Rusty stand at the entrance gate. 'It's his first show. But I do wish he'd calm down.'

'Try taking him to the quiet end of the field,' suggested Bernard. 'Trot some circles and figures of eight.'

Several other riders seemed to have had the same idea, and were schooling their ponies on the flat and jumping them over a practice jump that had been put up at one side of the field.

Bernard's suggestion ought to have worked. His theory was a sound one, and Penny knew that famous show jumpers had a work-out before going into the ring to take off their freshness and to make them concentrate and realize that they had a job to do. But, to Rusty, everything was new and exciting—the crowd, the fluttering bunting, the sudden blare of the loudspeaker and the other ponies trotting and cantering around.

So, instead of quietening down, Rusty seemed to get even more excited. He danced sideways, gave a couple of high-spirited bucks, and cantered on the spot.

'Under-fourteens in the ring, please,' came a voice over the loudspeaker, and Penny, with a sinking heart, rode Rusty to join the other competitors in the collecting-ring.

'Keep that pony away from mine,' warned a girl on a showy blue roan. 'I don't want Midnight to be kicked.'

Penny got even more flustered as she struggled to stop Rusty sidling and backing into the other ponies. Two competitors had already jumped, but she did not see their rounds, and it was only when the voice over the loudspeaker announced: 'The last competitor had eight faults. Will

Number Five come into the ring please?'—that she realized it was her turn to jump.

'This is it, Rusty,' she whispered urgently. 'Please, please try to calm down and think what you're doing.'

She knew she ought to ride quietly into the ring without any fuss so that her pony would go at a steady pace and take the jumps in his stride. But Rusty was not yet that sort of pony. He shot into the ring, and started to buck and Penny had to drive him on in a short circle to stop him bucking again.

'Ride him, cowgirl!' called a youth from the crowd, and Penny, blushing with shame, set Rusty at the jump.

Rusty raced at the obstacle, almost out of control, but the first jump was only a simple one and he cleared it without knocking it down. A post-and-rails lay ahead, and Rusty, even more excited with the triumph of the first jump behind him, fought Penny to increase his pace. Sooner than risk unbalancing him, Penny let him have his head, and somehow he managed to 'fly' the post-and-rails without fault. Now Penny had to swing him right-handed to come at the gate. The turn steadied Rusty enough to let him come at the obstacle correctly. A ripple of clapping from the crowd told Penny that they were safely over.

Now for the in-and-out. Here, Rusty's speed was his undoing. He landed too far over the first part of the jump and blundered into the second. Leaving it scattered behind him, he thundered on to the triple bars which also fell.

Penny swung him round and saw the stile ahead. She felt a sudden misgiving. It was as though she sensed Rusty was going to refuse, and not intending to let this happen, she dug in her heels, crouched forward and gave him a tap with her switch as she set him at the jump. Rusty seemed to leap forward and Penny felt sure he was going to take it.

Rusty's muscles tensed. Then, suddenly, remembering his fall at the last stile which he had been asked to jump, he swerved. Penny, taken completely by surprise, was thrown out of her saddle and clasped Rusty round the neck with both arms. A gasp came from the spectators, and Rusty hearing that vast 'Oh' thought that it was a sound of disapproval. Unnerved now, he threw Penny and galloped towards the edge of the ring. The crowd scattered and Rusty cleared the bales of hay that marked the barrier and bolted towards the gate.

In the ring Penny lay at the side of the jump, stunned, while two nurses, in Red Cross uniforms, and a steward hurried to her.

From the crowd ran Mr and Mrs Brooke. 'I knew something like this would happen.' Mrs Brooke, beside herself with anxiety, hardly knew what she was saying. 'We ought never to have let Penny and Jane take up show jumping, George. It's all our fault.'

FOURTEEN

Help from the Pony Club

'WHERE am I?' Penny opened her eyes near-
ly two hours later to find herself lying in her own bed at home
with her mother sitting in the chair at her bedside. Her head
was aching and she felt dizzy. 'What happened?'

'Lie still, dear.' Her mother's voice was comforting. 'You
fell off Rusty at the show, remember? You landed on your
head and you've had a slight concussion. Doctor Harrison's
been, and he says you must stay in bed for two or three days.'

A tap came at the bedroom door, and Jane's head appeared. 'I heard someone talking so I guessed Penny had
come round.' Jane's voice was hushed. 'May I come in?'

'Yes,' said Mrs Brooke. 'I'd like you to sit with Penny for
a few minutes, Jane, while I make her a warm drink.'

Mrs Brooke went downstairs and Penny turned to her
sister. 'What happened to Rusty?'

'After he'd thrown you he jumped into the crowd,' said
Jane, 'but luckily no one was hurt, and Major Kirkwood
managed to grab him. He's back in the field now.'

'And what happened to you and Freckles?' Penny asked.

'Nothing.' Jane's reply was rueful. 'We didn't get a chance
to jump. There was such a fuss over your mishap that the
jumping was held up for about half an hour, and then I had
to bring Rusty home. We'll be lucky if Mummy and Daddy
ever let us jump again after the fright you've given them.'

Penny looked at her sister in dismay.

'Oh, Jane, I've spoiled everything. How dreadful!'

'Are you going to stop me and Jane show jumping, Mummy?' Penny asked next morning when Mrs Brooke put the breakfast tray on her lap as she sat up in bed.

'I don't know, dear.' Mrs Brooke hesitated. 'You must admit that it can be dangerous. Another girl had a fall yesterday. She was quite a big girl, too, so Doctor Harrison tells me. She dislocated her shoulder, and he had to take her to the hospital to have it put back in place.'

'But, Mummy,' Penny pointed out, 'everybody's unlucky sometimes, and there are lots of people who've jumped in ever so many shows without getting hurt at all.'

'I dare say,' said Mrs Brooke, 'But I don't suppose their ponies are as temperamental as Rusty.'

'It's such a pity,' Penny sighed. 'Rusty's got real promise as a show jumper. David Leslie said so, and so did Madge Stevens. With practice he could compete at the big shows. He might even get to Wembley—to the Horse of the Year Show.'

'And pigs might fly,' said Mrs Brooke in a down-to-earth

way. 'Now stop day-dreaming and please don't let me hear any more about show jumping. I've had enough.'

'Straighten your hair quickly, dear.' Mrs Brooke moved from the bedroom window to pass a comb to Penny. 'You've got a visitor—Major Kirkwood. He's just driven up.'

Mrs Brooke hurried to answer the knock at the front door, and Penny sat up in bed, listening. Yes, Major Kirkwood was asking how she was. Mummy was now bringing him upstairs to see her, and, a moment later, Major Kirkwood was sitting on the bedside chair, and handing Penny a stack of pony magazines.

'Not lost your nerve, eh, young lady?' he asked with a smile.

'Oh no,' said Penny.

'I wish she had,' Mrs Brooke put in feelingly. 'Her father and I have lost ours! We're beginning to wonder whether we did right in letting her enter for the show, after all.'

'I see.' Major Kirkwood looked sympathetically at Mrs Brooke. 'Yes, it must have been a worrying time for you. But, you know, most of us have a tumble at some time or another, and Penny's a good little rider. She's not likely to come to much harm.'

'That's what I say,' said Penny. 'I wouldn't have fallen off on Saturday if Rusty hadn't been so afraid of the stile.'

She explained to Major Kirkwood how Rusty had landed on top of a sheep when jumping the stile out of Updean Woods.

'Ah, yes.' Major Kirkwood was thoughtful. 'It's possible that Rusty may be nervous of stiles for quite some time.'

'Yes, and the crowd upset him, too,' said Penny.

'It certainly did,' added her mother. 'Of course Rusty's only a young pony.'

'And the show was a new experience for him,' Major Kirkwood remarked.

'Anyway, it's not likely to happen again,' said Mrs Brooke. 'My husband and I don't want our daughters to do any more show jumping.'

'I suppose not.' Major Kirkwood sounded understanding. 'Now that's a natural reaction after a shock. But I do hope you'll change your mind.'

'I'm afraid that's not likely, Major Kirkwood,' said Mrs Brooke.

'Well then,' said Major Kirkwood helpfully, 'why not let someone else jump Rusty for a while—my niece, Cecilia would take him in hand for you, if you like.'

'That'd be wonderful,' exclaimed Penny. 'Rusty would have his chance after all.'

'Yes, and in the meantime,' said Major Kirkwood, 'Penny could borrow my old pony, Paddy. He's a Fell pony, quite sturdy and up to weight, but as steady as a rock. He's a sensible old fellow, is Paddy. What do you say, Mrs Brooke?'

'I don't know what to say.' Mrs Brooke looked from the Major to Penny and back. 'I don't want to wrap my children in cotton-wool, or make them afraid of their own shadows, but I'm still not happy about this show jumping.'

'Quite so,' nodded Major Kirkwood. 'Well, there's no need to make your mind up yet. Let Cecilia have Rusty and see how he goes on. Penny won't be doing any show jumping on old Paddy.'

Penny looked pleadingly at her mother.

'Please let me borrow Paddy,' she begged.

'Well, I suppose at least I should have the comfort of knowing that you won't even be riding Rusty until he's steadier.' She smiled gratefully at Major Kirkwood. 'Thank you for your kind offer.'

'It's a pleasure.' Major Kirkwood got up from the chair. 'Cecilia will ride Paddy over tomorrow and collect Rusty.'

So Rusty went to Cecilia's, and Paddy came to Orchard Cottage. Penny liked Cecilia as soon as she saw her. She was about her own age with curly hair, freckles and sunny blue eyes. Slim and neat, she looked every inch a rider. Penny felt sure Rusty would be in capable hands.

Jane and Freckles carried on practising with Bernard and Corker for the Pony Club Pairs, and, a few days later Penny was well enough to be up and about riding Paddy.

At the end of the week Penny telephoned Cecilia to ask how Rusty was progressing.

'He's jumping quite well,' Cecilia told her, 'but he's still not too happy about stiles, and I'm not forcing the pace. I shall try to get his confidence back gradually. I'm giving him some elementary dressage to supple him and make him more obedient.'

The following week Cecilia reported that she had now got Rusty jumping the stile without fuss, and that she was taking him to a small show the next Saturday at Birkdale, about thirty miles away.

'Daddy and I will be coming past the end of your lane with the horse-box so we'll take you with us.'

Penny was thrilled to see Rusty jumping. He seemed much steadier, and was not so upset by the crowd and the excitement of the show. He didn't win any rosettes, but Cecilia said he'd jumped quite well for his second time out.

'The third show will be Rusty's real test,' she told Penny as they travelled home in the cab of the horse-box.

'When will that be?' Penny wondered.

'I'm not sure,' said Cecilia. 'I want to do some more dressage to loosen him up, but, with luck, he may be ready to jump at Great Aston in a fortnight.'

FIFTEEN

The big show

HORSE-BOXES, pony trailers and riders on all kinds of horses and ponies were passing through the entrance gates of Great Aston town-field which had been temporarily converted to a showground.

There were refreshment tents, a secretary's booth, and a marquee set up by a local saddler and corn-merchant with displays of tack, and horse-and-pony foods. Flags were flying; the town band was playing rousing marches and a jostling crowd was making its way to the stands.

Penny jumped off the bus by the entrance gates, paid her shilling and hurried through the crowd in search of Cecilia and Rusty. This time Cecilia had not been able to give Penny a lift. A pony-breeder had asked Cecilia to ride two of her entries in the showing-classes and so Cecilia had ridden Rusty over to the pony-farm the previous evening, stayed the night, so as to put in some practice on the two ponies, and was coming on to the show with their owner.

Suddenly, Penny saw Cecilia riding up and down beside the hedge on a well-proportioned blue roan.

'Hello,' Penny called, running to them.

'Hello, Penny.' Cecilia reined up. 'Rusty's in the horse box with Topping Lady.' She patted the blue roan. 'This is Misty Dawn. I'm showing her in the Best Pony Class.' She dismounted and led the way to one of the large horse-boxes. 'Rusty's in here.'

Penny climbed into the horse-box and made a fuss of Rusty who seemed glad to see her. She gave him a handful of pony cubes and then led him down the ramp.

'He's looking well,' she told Cecilia. 'Steady, boy.' She took a firm grasp on Rusty's bridle as he danced sideways when another pony and rider trotted past.

'He's a bit fresh,' said Cecilia. 'I've been giving him oats. I want to do really well today.'

Rusty shifted his feet, snorted and shook his mane.

Just then a voice blared over the loudspeaker.

'Class number one in the ring.'

'That's me and Misty Dawn,' Cecilia told Penny. 'Will you hang on to Rusty until I come back? Saddle him and give him a bit of a work-out, to settle him down. I shan't be long.'

Saddling and bridling Rusty was no easy matter because he was so fit and on his toes. He kept shifting and throwing up his head, but at last Penny got his saddle and bridle into place and managed to make him stand long enough to pull up his nylon-girth and carefully to smooth it so as to ensure that his skin was not wrinkled or pinched between the strands.

'There you are, Rusty. That's comfortable, isn't it?' Penny said, patting her pony and gathering up her reins to mount.

Rusty stood just long enough for Penny to get into the saddle. Then he was off at a high-stepping trot while Penny did her best to keep him clear of other ponies and riders. She let him trot fast for a few minutes to work off some of his excess energy. Then she took a feel on his reins and sat down in the saddle.

Evidently Cecilia's dressage work had done some good because Rusty, immediately obedient, came to hand in a collected, cadenced trot. He was moving nicely, head bent at the poll and circling at a controlled pace when Cecilia, her class ended, came back with Misty Dawn, a red rosette on the pony's bridle.

'I've got to hurry,' she told Penny. 'Topping Lady's in the next class. So will you be an angel, Penny, and see to Misty Dawn? You'll find a wisp in the box. She needs rubbing down. She's got herself into a lather and I'm scared of her catching cold. Just loosen her saddle. Don't take it off.'

Penny tied up Rusty and was running Misty Dawn's stirrup irons up their leathers when Cecilia mounted Topping Lady and trotted off.

'It's your class next, Rusty.' Penny spoke over her shoulder to her pony as she wisped down Misty Dawn. She moved the coiled rope of hay over Misty Dawn's shoulders and flanks in a circular movement, talking to her soothingly, and trying not only to dry off the sweat, but to get the pony to relax as well. When Cecilia came back with another rosette Penny was standing on the ramp gently pulling the mare's ears.

'She started to shiver,' Penny told Cecilia, 'so I thought this might help to stop her catching cold.'

'Good for you,' Cecilia said. She got off Topping Lady and inspected Misty Dawn. 'She'll do now. We'll put a blanket over her saddle and put her into the box.'

When both Misty Dawn and Topping Lady were safely pulling at their hay nets, Cecilia turned to Penny. 'Now we'd better get Rusty into the collecting ring. The Under Fourteen-Two jumping has just begun.'

Rusty kept flicking his ears and turning his head as Cecilia, Penny running alongside, trotted him through the unfamiliar sights and sounds of the crowded showground. He danced sideways when a nearby loudspeaker crackled explosively before blaring the number of the first competitor. When they got to the collecting-ring he shied away from the assembled ponies. Undaunted, Cecilia closed her legs to his sides and drove him on. She rode him right to the rails where she could study the course and watch the other riders taking the jumps. Penny stood beside her, intently following a fair-haired girl in a brown crash-cap riding an elderly-looking but obviously very experienced faded-grey pony to clear jump after jump.

'Her timing's just right, and that pony never puts a foot wrong,' Cecilia told Penny. 'He's Grey Knight and the girl's Eleanor Robinson. Her two older sisters had him before she did. He must be quite fifteen, and now he seems better than ever.'

After a clear round, Grey Knight left the ring to applause, and a small ginger-haired boy cantered into the ring on a keen little Exmoor. The jumps were high for the Exmoor, but he was plucky and took them well. The boy rode him rather fast, but he never interfered with his mouth and let the pony judge his take-off for himself. They had only four faults as they swung into the middle of the course and galloped towards the Road Closed and the wall. The pony cleared the Road Closed but refused at the wall, and Penny watched closely to see what would happen next.

Suddenly she became aware of a bee buzzing round her head. She waved it away and saw, to her dismay, that it was about to settle on Rusty's neck. Cecilia saw it, too, and she and Penny both flapped their hands at it. Its steady buzz became an angry whine, and before Cecilia could brush it away it darted upwards, frightened, and as Cecilia bent forward, flew against her cheek.

'Oh, you stupid creature! Go away!' said Cecilia. Next moment she gave a cry of pain as the bee stung her just below her left eye. 'Ouch!' she exclaimed, raising her hand to her cheek.

'Don't rub it,' Penny said quickly. 'That'll only make it worse.'

'It's swelling,' said Cecilia, alarmed. 'I can feel it. My eye seems to be closing up.'

'Number forty-two into the ring, please,' blared a voice over the loudspeakers. 'Number forty-two.'

'That's Rusty's number,' said Cecilia. 'We shall have to go. But—oh gosh! I can hardly see out of this eye.'

Cecilia took her hand away from her eye to tighten her reins. Penny was shocked to see that Cecilia's cheek was red and puffy and that her eye was almost closed.

'Number forty-two into the ring,' insisted the voice over the loudspeaker. 'Hurry up, please. Number forty-two!'

'It's no use,' said Cecilia. 'I can't ride. My eye hurts too much.' She slid to the ground and gave Penny a push. 'Go on. You'll have to ride Rusty.'

'I can't,' said Penny. 'I'd only make a fool of myself. Rusty's so fresh.'

'Number forty-two,' insisted the voice over the loudspeaker. 'Is number forty-two anywhere on the ground?'

'Go on, Penny,' Cecilia thrust Rusty's reins into Penny's hand and held a stirrup for her to mount. 'You're keeping everyone waiting.'

SIXTEEN

A rosette for Rusty

WHEN Rusty felt Penny's weight on his back, he shot forward into the ring. Penny found her off-stirrup and steadied him. The voice over the loudspeaker announced her number.

Rusty's pace increased as Penny set him at the first jump. It was a simple brushwood fence with a log on the take-off side, and he cleared it with inches to spare. He was going much too fast, thought Penny, as they cantered on towards the gate. This time there was no log in front. It was a straight up-and-down—one of the most difficult obstacles for a pony to jump.

'Steady, Rusty!' Penny took a pull on the reins. Thanks to Cecilia's schooling, Rusty obediently slowed his pace. 'That's it.' Penny put a hand on his neck. 'Now, have a good look at the jump.'

Rusty's ears flickered back; then pointed forward. He seemed to size up the gate. Up and over he went, in a perfectly-timed leap. Penny swung him right-handed. He cleared another brushwood fence and, as the crowd clapped, he broke into a gallop. Ahead lay the first fence of the in-and-out.

'Not so fast, Rusty.'

Penny steadied him. The in-and-out must be taken at a steady pace. If a pony rushed it, he might land too far over the first jump and so not be properly placed for the second. Checking his pace in response to Penny's pressure on the bit, Rusty came at the first fence just right, cleared it, gathered himself together and took the second.

Now for the triple-bar. But triples had never worried Rusty. He had a naturally good scope and the flight of three bars was just what he needed fully to extend himself. There was a gasp from the spectators as he cleared the jump. Next —the stile! Penny's heart thumped, but she tried not to let her nervousness show itself to Rusty.

Driving him forward determinedly with her legs, she set him at the jump.

Again Cecilia's schooling showed. Rusty flicked back his ears, though he gave no other sign of his fear. He took the jump well; then he broke into a gallop on landing as though he was glad to be safely over. Penny slowed him when he came to the parallel bars.

Rusty shook his head, disliking the pressure on his bit. Penny held him back until they were a couple of strides from the jump, then she let him go, and Rusty's sudden burst of speed carried him well over. Penny swung him

left-handed towards the cross-barrier of the Road Closed. This was a difficult obstacle because, to get through without touching it, one had to take the jump exactly in the middle. Rusty kept straight, cleared it and sped on to the final wall amidst applause. There was a gasp as he rose to the wall and Penny thought he had touched it. She looked back as Rusty cantered towards the exit, but nothing fell.

'Number forty-two had a clear round,' the voice over the loudspeaker announced.

'Good pony, Rusty.'

Penny jumped down and gave him some pony nuts as she led him back to the collecting-ring where Cecilia was being tended by a St John's Ambulance man in a black-and-white uniform. Cecilia squirmed away from the pad of cotton-wool that the man was holding to her eye, and turned to Penny.

'Well done,' she said. 'You rode Rusty splendidly. Now you'll have to jump it off with Grey Knight for first place.'

'Keep still, missy,' begged the St John's man, trying to place the cotton-wool pad over Cecilia's eye. 'I've got the sting out: so the worst of it's over.'

By the time that Rusty and Penny were called into the ring for the jump-off, Cecilia, with the pad of cotton-wool bandaged over her left eye, was standing at the rail to watch.

'Good luck!' she called, as Penny cantered Rusty into the ring.

The veteran Grey Knight had successfully cleared all four of the jumps which had been raised for the jump-off. Another competitor—a boy on a dark-bay children's hunter, had also had a clear round and was yet to jump-off, so Penny knew that Rusty must clear all the jumps if he was to stand a chance of winning.

The four jumps to be taken were the gate, now standing at three feet six, the triple at three feet nine, the Road Closed, and the wall to which had been added an extra row of 'bricks'. The jumps looked formidable, and Penny's heart sank a little, but she pulled herself together and tried to feel confident as she set Rusty at the gate. He cleared it and cantered on to sail over the triple. He seemed to be enjoying himself and gave a pleased buck as he approached the Road Closed. He did not come at this quite right, but somehow he managed to straighten himself in mid-air and did not touch any part of the jump. Penny collected him again and urged him to an extra burst of speed to enable him to get the necessary height as he raced for the wall.

Rusty rose like a bird, tucked-up his forefeet well and seemed to sail through the air. So Penny was surprised to hear a sharp gasp from the crowd as three 'bricks' fell. Four faults. Whatever happened now they could not win.

'You might still be second,' comforted Cecilia as Penny halted Rusty again in the collecting-ring.

But the boy, cool and calm on the immaculate dark bay, got round without any faults. So he and Grey Knight were called in equal firsts and both received red rosettes while Penny, as third, got a yellow one.

With the rosette between her teeth, Penny followed Grey Knight and the dark bay as they galloped round the ring. When they came back into the collecting-ring, she reined up and dismounted. Taking the yellow rosette from between her teeth, she fastened it to Rusty's bridle.

'There!' she patted him. 'Your first rosette. You're a real show jumper now.' She hugged him. 'You're a good pony, Rusty. You jumped beautifully, and you didn't play-up over the stile.' She buried her face in his mane. 'Oh, Rusty, I do love you.'

An hour and a half later Penny led Rusty down the ramp of the horse-box outside Orchard Cottage.

'Goodbye, Penny,' Cecilia called from the window of the cab as the driver fastened up the ramp and climbed back inside. 'See you at the next show.'

'I hope so,' Penny said, waving back before turning to lead Rusty up the path. She did not feel as confident as she sounded. What would Mummy and Daddy have to say when they learned that she had jumped Rusty in the show after all?

'Hi, Penny!' Jane, having heard Rusty's hooves on the path, came running out, followed by Mr and Mrs Brooke. 'Goodness!' Jane exclaimed catching sight of the rosette on Rusty's headpiece. 'Well done, Cecilia. It was sporting of her to let you have the rosette, although I suppose she's got dozens at home. She's always winning.'

Penny broke into a broad smile. She could not contain her delight any longer.

'It wasn't Cecilia's rosette. It's mine; I won it,' she told them proudly. 'I rode Rusty.'

Aware of the alarmed look on her mother's face, Penny went on to explain what had happened. '. . . And Rusty behaved perfectly, Mummy,' she assured her. 'You wouldn't have felt at all nervous if you'd been there and seen him. He loves shows now. He was a bit excited to begin with, but he soon settled down. Cecilia says that he's got just the right temperament for show jumping. She said I might as well bring him home because there was nothing left for her to teach him. What he needs now, Cecilia says, is more experience, and practice. His scope will increase as his muscles get stronger.'

'I see,' Mr Brooke said quietly.

'Yes,' said Penny. 'It's up to Rusty and me now.'

'I should have thought it was up to your mother and me,' Mr Brooke said with feeling.

'Up to us!' Mrs Brooke echoed. 'I think it's *beyond* us.'

'Exactly.' Mr Brooke sounded defeated as he turned to his wife. 'Whatever are we going to do now?'

'Goodness knows!' Mrs Brooke looked ceilingwards as though for guidance. 'I suppose we shall just have to make the best of it and try not to worry too much.'

Just then Rusty pushed his head against her arm. He wanted to be fussed.

'A show jumper in the family,' Penny's mother said, patting him. 'Well, I suppose we've just got to get used to the idea.' She rubbed the white star between Rusty's eyes and stroked his soft muzzle. 'Mind you take good care of Penny, you rascal!'